Simply Nanju

Read more for middle-grade readers from Duckbill

Simply Nanju

Zainab Sulaiman

duckbill

Duckbill Books and Publications Pvt Ltd
F2 Oyster Operaa, 35/36 Gangai Street, Kalakshetra Colony,
Besant Nagar, Chennai 600090
www.duckbill.in
platypus@duckbill.in

First published by Duckbill Books 2016
Text copyright © Zainab Sulaiman 2016

Zainab Sulaiman asserts the moral right to be identified
as the author of this work.

10 9 8 7 6 5 4 3

ISBN 978-93-83331-70-3

Typeset by PrePSol Enterprises Pvt. Ltd.

Printed at Thomson Press (India) Ltd.

Also available as an ebook

Children's reading levels vary widely. The general reading levels
are indicated by colour on the back cover. There are three levels:
younger readers, middle readers and young adult readers. Within
each level, the position of the dot indicates the reading complexity.
Books for young adults may contain some slightly mature material.

Monday, 7 July

Nanju poked his head out of the last stall of the bathroom, and gave his khaki shorts one firm tug to make sure everything inside was secure. He peered around to see if the coast was clear.

A plastic packet with a pair of soiled school shorts lay tucked away under the stone ledge of the stall, hidden among the cleaning detergents, mops and brooms that the Ayammas stored there. Nanju had decided to come back for his packet when school was over.

Wearing a diaper did not bother Nanju very much. Though he was ten years old, it was as normal for him as pulling on a pair of socks or lacing up one's sneakers was for other kids. Because his crooked feet turned inwards, pulling on socks or lacing up sneakers were not things Nanju did.

Nanju's parents had told him that the doctor in the Mahegowda Government Hospital had said that there was something wrong with his spine soon after he was born.

'He won't know when to go to bathroom!' Nanju imagined the doctor barking—doctors in government hospitals always spoke to their patients as if they were deaf. 'Must always wear nappy!'

The school Ayammas didn't appreciate stumbling over Nanju's little parcels, and they were known to tweak ears and pinch bottoms if it took their fancy.

Nanju couldn't afford to be caught with dirty pants again. Theresa Miss had promised to call his father if he forgot to check his diaper in the breaks and had another accident.

Since he had entered Standard Five, life had changed. He had just one year left before he moved up into Standard Six, the big year at the United Integrated School. After that, one had to prove one's competence to be given admission to a new school.

'Learn to be responsible!' was the new mantra. And no one took this more seriously than Appa.

'This year you must get good marks, Nanju,' Appa had glared at him that very morning.

Nanju decided that the glare was because Appa could not find his tailor's tape and chalk piece and was swearing under his breath as he searched.

'They're on top of the TV, Appa,' he said cheerfully, sprawled out on the floor as he put on his calipers, the plastic encasings for his bent legs that gave him additional support when he walked. 'Shanti Akka always puts it there.'

His father rewarded him with a deeper scowl. Since his wife had died two years earlier, his daughter Shanti had taken to arranging his things for him. But he could never find them.

'Don't change the topic! If you score badly this year, I'm going to send you to Kolar, I promise you!'

Prakash Mama ran a hostel for orphan boys in Kolar. Nanju always felt like a mouse in a lion's den when Prakash Mama dragged them around the hostel on their annual visits. The rough-looking inmates were usually engaged in tearing each other's shirts off on the dusty football field, or hanging the smaller fellows face downwards from the monkey bars, or simply baring their teeth in obscene grins at the scared creature that crept along beside Prakash Mama. Nanju would try to ignore the jeers and hisses that filled his ears from all sides.

How could Appa threaten to send him off to this place?

What Nanju needed to do now was to get across the long corridor without anyone seeing him. On one side were the classrooms, and on the other, big wide windows that overlooked the small courtyard where the kids ate and played. All was quiet; the children seemed to be safely tucked away in their classrooms. The coast was clear for him to leave.

He hurried out of the bathroom, and hobbled slap bang into the arms of the oldest school Ayamma.

'Ay! Go slow! And what are you doing hanging around in the bathroom during class? Don't tell me you've again ...'

'No, Amma, nothing! Just going to toilet ...' Nanju wiggled his head from side to side.

Ayamma gave him a long look. Her lips tightened and her mouth curled up a little.

Nanju raced off before she could reply, wiping his wet hands on his shorts. He had washed his hands thoroughly in order to get the smell off, and as he hadn't used any soap, it had taken a lot of water to do the job.

He would have normally slowed down once he was safely out of sight of the Ayamma, and taken his own sweet time to get back to class. But this morning, Theresa Miss had had a surprise for him: he was to join a group of his classmates who would spent one period every morning practising reading—under the trees, in the courtyard—with a new assistant teacher. Nanju was looking forward to an hour in the late-morning sunshine.

He found the little group settled on two stone benches under a shady frangipani tree. A generous stone table that was rooted between the benches was the common desk.

The new Miss was reading something out of a blue book with gold designs. The cover had a picture of a giant man straining under the weight of the sky that was resting on his shoulders.

'Miss, Theresa Miss said to join your group,' Nanju interrupted.

'Come, join in,' the young woman gestured to him to come closer. 'What's your name?'

'Nanjegowda,' Nanju answered, perching himself at the edge of the bench.

'What's your name, Miss? Forgot ...' Mahesh craned his head up and grinned, exposing a set of very big, very white teeth.

Mahesh was Nanju's best friend. He was leaning forward in his wheelchair, his upper body resting against the stone bench on which the others were sitting.

Mahesh had an enormous head and a small torso, with small twisted limbs. He always used a wheelchair in school—though he could crawl to get around—and he was also about quarter the size of his classmates. Mahesh was exceptionally smart, something that most people tended to overlook when they first saw him. He was in the reading group because he missed a lot of school due to frequent illnesses, and Theresa Miss thought extra practice would keep him up to speed.

'My name is Asha.'

'Where you come from, Miss?' Ronit piped up, his small beady eyes taking in Asha Miss's jet-black hair and almond-shaped eyes.

Ronit, small, shrewd and sprightly, was Nanju's nemesis. A few years earlier, Ronit had been trailing his arm outside a bus that was taking his mother and him home; another bus, in a hurry to overtake them, had brushed past and crushed his arm. It now hung useless at his side. Ronit, however, had another appendage that more than made up for the loss of this one—a nose for people's weaknesses. He could sniff them out a mile away. Nanju, reeking of a simplicity bordering on idiocy, was an easy target.

'I'm from Nagaland. Now let's get on with the story.'

Nanju turned his attention back to Asha Miss as her clear voice filled the silent shady courtyard:

'"Take back the sky?" said Atlas to Hercules. "Absolutely not! I have held it for a thousand years. And now I shall only come back after another thousand!"'

Asha Miss waved her arms about and her eyes widened as she described Hercules's horror when he realised that Atlas had tricked him. Nanju's eyes wandered off as he wondered what Shanti Akka had packed for lunch: he hoped it wasn't upma.

Ronit and his neighbour were fighting a silent battle over a rusty old battery. Ronit held it under the table in a tightly-clenched fist which the other boy was trying to pry open with both hands. They kept their eyes fixed firmly on the new Miss.

Mahesh sat back in his wheelchair and his extra-large head lolled on the leather headrest. He couldn't sit upright for more than ten minutes at a time.

Asha Miss stopped reading and looked around the group. Five sets of wide eyes stared back at her.

Maybe she can't understand the story either, Nanju thought, as Asha Miss suddenly looked a little lost.

'I think you children should read something from your textbooks,' she said, closing the blue book.

'I—ave—to—go—to—the—ouse.' Ronit read loudly and slowly from his English language reader.

'Not "ave", say "have".'

'Ave.'

'Have.'

Asha Miss held her palm up to her mouth and gently blew an H on it.

'Have,' he said, copying her and blowing onto his palm.

'Very good.'

Soon everyone was blowing on their palms, even as they continued to drop their Hs.

'Aradhana! Stop talking and sit down!' Theresa Miss thundered. It was the last period for the day and the children were restless.

The class teacher of Standard Five was middle-aged, with salt-and-pepper hair and a dignified way of pulling her saree pallu across her shoulders. At the moment, however, Theresa Miss resembled a tired old crow with a sore throat.

'Miss, I found my science book! It was on Armaan's wheelchair.' Aradhana sat down obediently, though she couldn't resist having the last word, as usual.

The class topper's books had been vanishing and reappearing ever since the start of the term and was a source of great sorrow for her and a joyful distraction for everybody else.

'Armaan! Why did you take her book?' Theresa Miss rounded on the culprit, who had dozed off in his wheelchair.

'What, Miss?' Armaan woke with a start. 'What, Miss?'

Armaan loved any kind of attention, because he rarely got any. He spent most of his day listening to the teacher or doing simple sums—one plus one, two plus four—in the only notebook he owned. Hence, he was always ready to engage in conversation, even where he was being rebuked. Armaan had cerebral palsy, which affects a part of the brain that controls movement. He couldn't move his legs, and his hand movements were also very limited.

'Nothing!' Too late, Theresa Miss realised who she was dealing with.

'Take out your science books and turn to Chapter Two. Today, I am going to teach you about molecules.'

Nanju scrambled about in his bag, looking for his dog-eared science textbook. He dreaded the next forty minutes but he was also relieved that Aradhana had found her notebook. Nanju had great respect for the pretty, popular Aradhana, who had stood first in class ever since he could remember.

'Miss should scold Armaan nicely, no, Mahesh?' Nanju bent down and whispered to his neighbour.

Mahesh used a chair and desk that was half the size of the regular classroom furniture, so that his feet could touch the ground. They both sat in the front row, to ensure that Mahesh was able to see the blackboard clearly, and Nanju could be right next to his lifeline.

'Miss should scold Armaan nicely, no, Mahesh?' Ronit mocked from his seat behind Nanju and the children sitting around him giggled.

'Shutyamouth!'

'You shut your mouth!'

'Miss! They're saying bad words,' one of the sneaker-pots shouted and the conversation came to an end.

Nanju seethed as Theresa Miss droned on about atoms and elements and compounds. He suspected that one of the titters had been Aradhana's, and he racked his brain to find a way to get back at Ronit. He was soon thick in the midst of a sweet revenge scene: Ronit had been publicly marched off to join Standard Three for his stupidity ... No, even that was too good for him. Nanju relocated him to the kindergarten, where he was forced to sit amongst the smelly pukey babies and write A-B-C-D a hundred times in his notebook.

A strange tickling feeling froze further daydreams.

'Don't move, Nanju! There's something on your neck,' a voice hissed from behind.

Theresa Miss was writing something on the board, lost in a steady stream of scientific dialogue.

'Eh what!' Nanju started to turn, but Ronit grabbed Nanju's shoulder with his good hand.

'Don't move! It'll bite!'

Nanju paused, unsure whether to call his enemy's bluff, or to risk being bitten.

A muffled laugh gave him his answer and he spun around angrily.

A grubby pigeon feather lay on Ronit's desk and Ronit stuck his tongue out at Nanju. Nanju could see Aradhana trying to keep a straight face.

'Nanju! Look in front and concentrate!' Theresa Miss yelled.

There was nothing to be done but to look in front and concentrate.

'Ay Nanju, copy these answers,' Mahesh's soft voice drifted up to him a few minutes later. 'Theresa Miss has given this for homework, but I've finished. And afterwards, we can have bubblegum—Goomer. I brought one for you also.'

Nanju swallowed his tears and nodded. Goomer was his favourite. Somehow, Mahesh always knew how to make him feel better.

A little while later, Theresa Miss hauled up Ronit for playing with a blade and Nanju cheered up. Ronit had carved his name into his wooden desk, and hence couldn't defend himself against the allegation.

Then the bell rang.

Nanju bounded off to the toilet as fast as he could, to retrieve his plastic packet before anyone else got to it. He breathed easier when he found it where he had left it, tucked away under the stone bench. He closed the door of the stall and tied the neck of the plastic bag into a clumsy knot and stuffed it deep into his schoolbag.

He was glad he had carried a change; some days he forgot.

He held his bag up to his nose and sniffed. Nothing. He did it once more to be sure. The smell of slightly sour curd-rice mingled with musty old schoolbag wafted into his nostrils.

Nanju did his final diaper check and headed to the courtyard where the regular rush of hurrying, hobbling, walker-pushing, wheelchair-racing children were enjoying the last few moments of freedom. A small damp patch on the back of his khaki shorts was the only sign of his recent adventures.

He clambered into the van and squeezed into the front seat next to Mahesh. Mahesh always sat right up front by the driver because he was so much smaller than all the others.

'Last! Last!'

Nanju popped his head out of the window and jeered at one of his van buddies, who lurched towards the van in jerky little steps, leaning on his walker for support.

The boy shook a fist at Nanju, lost his balance, and almost fell.

'Stop it, Nanjegowda!' shouted one of the teachers on van duty.

Nanju grinned and sat back. He gave Mahesh a friendly nudge in the ribs, Mahesh nudged him back; the driver shouted at everyone to 'Be quiet or else!' The engine roared to life and the van drove out of the gate and down the road.

Thursday, 10 July

'Armaan! Come to the side.' The prefect clicked his fingers.

Nanju leapt out of line and pushed Armaan's wheelchair towards the tall scowling boy, who was standing beside a ragtag bunch of violators—dirty uniforms, scruffy shoes, filthy nails—lined up at one side of the courtyard.

'If you come one more time without socks, I'll send you home! You understand?'

The barefoot boy stared at a crack in the ground and nodded.

'Go now!'

Nanju gave the boy a grateful smile. He was rewarded with a frown, but for Nanju this was a sign of the real thing. A true-blue prefect is one who isn't swayed by big gratuitous grins or flattering words or cheap gifts of bubblegum.

The prefect turned his attention to the other offenders, and Nanju wheeled Armaan off to class.

'Eh, Armaan, why can't your mother make you wear socks! Every day the prefects must tell you or what?' Nanju lectured Armaan, who sat quietly with a pinched look on his face.

Armaan couldn't wear shoes as his feet bent inwards, but he was supposed to wear a pair of long blue socks to school. But between him and her five other children—his mother barely had time to haul him to the van every morning and toss him into it—frivolities like socks were invariably sacrificed. And so Armaan had learnt to live with being pulled up every once in a while by the prefects.

Nanju, however, adored the prefects.

One had to be in Standard Six to be a prefect, and even then, there was no guarantee that one would be chosen for this illustrious position. The prefects were stationed all over school during assembly, and snack and lunch breaks. They watched over the noisy boisterous rabble with hawks' eyes and contemptuous lips.

Nanju and Armaan entered class just in time: a fight had broken out at the back of the classroom between the new boy Pratik and the Class Monitor.

Nanju dumped a protesting Armaan up front and elbowed his way to the back for a better view. The Class Monitor, who was the bigger of the two, had pinned his opponent to the floor.

'Say sorry!' the Class Monitor panted.

'Leave! Leave me!'

The Class Monitor responded by pressing his knee down harder on Pratik's chest.

'Stop it!' Theresa Miss entered the room out of breath and in a bad mood. 'Behave yourselves!'

'He only, Miss!' the Class Monitor whined, getting off Pratik. 'He only pushed first.'

'No, Miss! He said ...' Pratik fell silent.

'I don't care what he said!' Theresa Miss barked. 'New boy, and already fighting, eh? And what's happened to your nose?'

Pratik had a round face with round shining eyes like jamuns. An ink-blue bruise was spread across the generous ridge of his nose.

'Nothing, Miss,' Pratik mumbled, returning to his seat in the front row, beside Nanju.

Pratik's family had recently moved to Bangalore from a small town in Tamil Nadu and his father had requested Theresa Miss to help him settle down. Theresa Miss thought the best way to help was to have him sitting right under her own, slightly slimmer, nose.

'Must have got belted somewhere. Serves him right!' the Class Monitor muttered under his breath.

The fight had started because he had asked Pratik the very same question (a couple times more than Theresa Miss) and had finally been rewarded with a shove.

'Take out your maths books and start working.' Theresa Miss began to fill the board with nasty multiplication sums.

'Miss, my book is missing again,' Aradhana called out in her high thin voice, her head in her desk as she rummaged around for her notebook.

Theresa Miss watched grimly as Aradhana twice turned her bag inside out and got down on her hands and knees and searched under the tables and chairs around her.

'Did you have it yesterday?' Theresa Miss demanded finally.

'Yes, Miss.'

'Then where is it? You blamed Armaan the other day ... no, don't deny it now.' Theresa Miss waved a protesting Aradhana down. 'And now it's disappeared into thin air, I suppose? And you all! Search in your desks! Maybe one of you has taken her book.'

But the book didn't turn up. Aradhana had to make do with a double sheet of paper that Theresa Miss tore out from an old book.

'Just because you come first don't think you can behave any way you want in my class, do you hear? I expect you to copy down all the notes when you find your book. Careless girl!'

Nanju bit his lip as Aradhana tried very hard not to cry. Who could be taking her books, he wondered. It had to be somebody very stupid, since they must be taking the books to copy down the notes written in the neatest handwriting he had ever seen.

'All those who got full marks, put your hands up.' Theresa Miss was handing out the spelling test papers.

A few hands shot up, Pratik's amongst them. But what shocked Nanju more was that Aradhana's hand wasn't amongst them. He darted a quick look at her and was sorry that he had done so: she was staring down at her desk, a miserable look on her face. It's all those missing books, Nanju thought. Aradhana had never scored anything but top marks in living memory.

Terrible Thursdays meant open humiliation and Nanju braced himself for what was to come next.

'And all those who scored zero—stand up! Not you, Armaan—put your hand down,' Theresa Miss ordered Armaan, whose hand had immediately gone up, as he couldn't stand up.

Armaan followed a simpler syllabus from the rest of the class, and did not need to take the tests. But he liked to be an active participant in all activities and wasn't about to be left behind here either. He put his hand down, looking disappointed.

Nanju wondered whether he should try his luck and not stand up. After all, it wasn't necessary that he scored zero in every test. But he had forgotten about Ronit.

'Hah! Can't even spell "left"!' Ronit screeched, leaning forward and looking over Nanju's shoulder. Nanju had written 'felt'.

And so muttering a subdued 'Shutyamouth', Nanju, the only one to have got all ten words wrong, had no choice but to stand up.

'Continue this way, Nanjegowda—and you can get ready to bring your father in very soon.' Theresa Miss turned her attention to Ronit who was jerking his shoulders up and down in short sharp staccato moves, the latest Tamil hit playing in his head.

Nanju sank down into his chair, relieved that he had got off so easily. He made a mental note to leave the test paper behind in his desk, and went back to joining the dots on the picture at the back of the new notebook Appa had bought for him.

To Nanju's distaste, Ronit was relocated to the first row and he squeezed himself in between Pratik and Nanju. Nanju could see Ronit taking in Pratik's shiny green-and-black mesh bag with the words 'Ben 10' scrawled over it. Ben was punching the air with his left arm, all the better to show off his big fat Ben 10 watch.

Ronit's eyes were focussed on the plastic suitcase-like handle that stuck out of the back of the bag, and the sleek steel wheels.

'Nice bag, man,' Ronit whispered to Pratik.

'My Daddy bought,' Pratik whispered back. A look of shared appreciation for the finer things in life passed between the boys.

Theresa Miss shouted something about not allowing people to play during snack break if they didn't complete their work, and everyone began to act busy.

'Ay Ronit, did you take my rubber?'

Nanju had finished. He had copied all Mahesh's answers, as usual, and was clearing up.

'No. And what's that smell?'

Ronit raised his head in the air and sniffed like a bloodhound hot on a trail. He caught Pratik's eye and raised his eyebrows questioningly. Pratik gave a tiny nod.

Nanju, who had discovered that his eraser was in his pocket after all, stared straight ahead in a determined fashion.

'Miss! Smell coming, Miss.'

Ronit put his good hand up to announce this find; his eyes gleamed. Pratik looked down and tried to hide a smirk.

'What smell?' Theresa Miss turned to Ronit.

'Dirty smell, Miss!' Ronit couldn't keep the grin off his face any longer.

'It's coming from outside!' Theresa Miss glared at him, taking in Nanju's air of strained indifference. 'And have you finished your work? Or are you fooling around as usual?'

Before Ronit could reply, the snack bell rang.

'Sit down!' Theresa Miss ordered, as thirty little bottoms began to twitch. 'I have an announcement to make.'

'So what are you going to do?' Mahesh asked Nanju during snack break.

'Don't know ...'

The school always celebrated its Annual Day in August with a Talent Show. The children could take part in a fancy-dress competition or perform a short act, either individually or in a group. There were prizes in all categories.

Aradhana and her friends were arguing about which song they should sing. One of the girls wanted to go with the latest hit, 'I want to kiss you ... kiss you ... kiss you ...' but Aradhana felt that Theresa Miss might not appreciate it.

Nanju was toying with the idea of participating. He loved prizes and had never won one in his entire life.

As he gave his nose a thorough dig, Nanju pondered the matter. Maybe he could sing ... but he knew his voice was no good. He had no talent as a dancer, either, and the plastic calipers that were wrapped around his legs didn't really help. And he had nothing to wear for the fancy-dress competition. What could he possibly do?

Kevin hummed softly to himself as he waited outside the principal's office.

'Stop it!' his class teacher glared at him. 'Don't think you're too smart!'

Kevin pretended not to hear and looked out of the window that opened on to the courtyard. He could see the new teacher taking class for a bunch of Standard Fives. He decided to join them after he had finished.

His class teacher was muttering under her breath as they waited. 'One of these days I'm going to go into labour and have this baby here! And it will all be this boy's fault!'

She glared at Kevin as she massaged the small of her back.

'And this is not the first time, ma'am, he's always back-answering! Now the others are also starting to behave like him. Look at him! Even now he's not bothered!'

Principal had called them in and Kevin was studying the white board that was hanging on one of the walls with great interest. On it was emblazoned:

'Teachers must submit all reports by 3pm today.
NO excuses will be accepted!'

'So, Kevin, what is this I hear?' Principal growled at him from behind her thick-rimmed glasses.

She was a short, squat lady with a round face and a preference for stripey silk sarees. She looked a little like a bulldog swaddled in a circus tent.

'What, Miss? What I did?' Kevin turned to her with an expression of wide-eyed innocence on his nut-brown face.

'What what?' The bulldog almost leapt out of her seat. 'Do you enjoy coming here every second day? You're in Standard Six, not in KG. Learn to behave!'

Kevin's eyes strayed to the window: the new Miss was showing the students a video on her phone. Then his ears pricked up. The principal was finally saying something important.

'One more complaint and I won't let you play in the match next Friday, you hear? Now go to class and behave yourself!'

'Okay, Miss!'

Kevin was the captain of the school cricket team and he meant to win the upcoming friendly match between United and the Nethra School for the Hearing Impaired.

Nethra came over every year to play a cricket match that so far, much to the hosts' humiliation, they had lost every year.

'And tell your aunty to come and see me,' the principal added. 'Your mother's still not here, I presume?'

'No, Miss. In Dubai.'

Kevin's mother worked as a housemaid in Dubai and his father was a drunk who had made himself comfortable on the street and rarely visited the boy. Kevin lived with an aunt, who had children—and many problems—of her own.

Ramappa the gardener, who also doubled up as the school watchman, had told the principal that a couple of rough-looking teenagers from the nearby slum had dropped by school one evening to look Kevin up. 'He was asking them if everything was okay,' Ramappa had smiled drily. 'Like he's some big rowdy or something.'

'Okay, go now,' the principal dismissed Kevin and told his sulky teacher that she'd look into it.

'Look into it ... my foot!' Kevin's teacher mumbled as she waddled across the courtyard to her class.

Friday, 18 July

Nanju was a genius at forgetting things. Most of the time, these were things that deserved forgetting—homework, notes that needed to be completed, a complaint letter from Theresa Miss to Appa.

But this time he had forgotten to leave his spelling test paper behind in school and Appa had found it a week later, scrunched up at the bottom of his bag. The paper was scoured with red crosses, a big fat zero blinking like a red light at the end.

'Appa, I'm ...'

Appa looked up, and Nanju's voice died in his throat. Behind the wall that separated the kitchen from the rest of their one-room house, Shanti Akka tried to be as quiet as possible as she washed up the morning's utensils.

'I studied, Appa ...' Nanju tried again, but his father cut him off.

'I'm sending you off, Nanju,' he said. He got up slowly, as if he were carrying something very heavy, and walked towards the hooks on the wall where the family hung their clothes. 'I'm sending you to Prakash Mama.' He reached into his pocket and pulled out his battered old phone.

'No Appa!' Nanju burst into tears and ran towards his father.

But Appa pushed him aside, and Nanju fell backwards on the bed he shared with Shanti Akka, and until a while ago, with his Amma. Appa always slept on a mattress on the floor.

'Please, Appa! I promise I'll study properly,' Nanju's wails filled the small room.

'Appa, give him one more chance ...' Shanti Akka asked in her most pleading voice. 'I'll help him this time. Amma always ...'

'Now you don't start!' Appa turned on Shanti and she looked down quickly. 'Your mother spoilt him all her life and look what it's got us! And your wonderful Prakash Mama also won't ever pick up his phone!'

Appa wanted to fling his mobile to the ground, but as it had cost him half his monthly wages—even though it was a bit of second-hand junk—he thought better of it. Instead, he flung his vest onto the floor and Shanti dutifully picked it up.

'I'll study, Appa! Really! Please don't send me to the hostel!' Nanju continued to weep, the tears cutting grimy tracks down his round face. If only Amma was here, he thought, she would never allow Appa to send him away.

'Please Appa ... I'll help him, I promise,' his sister spoke up again.

It was getting late for Shanti. She was in Standard Nine and had special preparatory classes in the morning. She would be punished if she arrived late for them. But she couldn't bring herself to leave till she was sure Appa had changed his mind. Nanju was the world's most annoying brother, but Shanti couldn't imagine life without him.

Appa picked up his lunchbox and walked to the door.

'One last time, Nanju,' he said, turning at the doorway and fixing his eyes on his son, who was wiping his overflowing nose on his sleeve.

'One more time ... and you're gone.'

'Better pay attention in class now!' Shanti Akka gave Nanju's ear a sharp tweak as she rushed him through the door and locked it. 'Promise?'

And from the bottom of his heart, Nanju promised that he would pay attention and ask all the right questions and copy down his homework and be the most diligent student that ever lived.

'Kevin! Why aren't you bowling properly?' His class teacher shouted at Kevin from where she was watching the match under a shady tree, resting her sore back against the trunk. Some of the other teachers were with her.

Kevin looked around with a haunted expression. He had just bowled a wide. He rolled the ball in his hands as he tried to decide where to place his fielders.

Then he spotted Asha Miss sitting among a bunch of rowdy third graders.

She gave him a big smile and a two-handed thumbs-up.

This time, he bowled a good length.

The batsman from the rival team defended the ball, but didn't dare take a run.

The cricket match had witnessed a good turnout. Though only a few of the children were actively participating—they would get their chance at the Special Sports Day that was to follow shortly—teachers and pupils alike were happy to spend an afternoon basking in the warm July sunshine.

The cricket match was the best kind of holiday. It was perfectly legitimate to fool around with one's friends and misbehave all afternoon. No one could do anything more than throw you an annoyed look.

United had won the toss and had chosen to bat. They had notched up a grand total of forty runs. The Nethra School for the Hearing Impaired had come on with a swagger: forty runs was a pathetic score in a ten-over match, and marked a new low even for United.

But then Nethra began to lose wickets, until it finally came down to their tall, handsome captain and one last player. They had scored a paltry ten runs off the first six overs, and now needed thirty-one runs off the next twenty-four balls to win the game. The situation looked hopeless.

Then their school captain began to hit one boundary after another. Now, all Nethra needed to win were twelve runs off the last six balls

Kevin cracked his knuckles and ordered his fielders to move back.

The fielders dutifully complied. From his new position in the playground, Ronit spotted Asha Miss and waved at her. Pratik, however, was still standing in his old position, scuffing his shoes against a big rock, oblivious to what was going on.

Kevin took one last look around the field, took a deep breath, and ran up to bowl.

Nanju's face reflected a new seriousness. He sat on the bench, bag beside him, deep in contemplation.

'I say it's Armaan!' he burst out. 'Remember how Aradhana's science book was found on his wheelchair last week? And the other book that went missing on Thursday was found without its cover in the dustbin today? He sits close to her—he could easily have done it.'

All memories of the showdown Nanju had had with Appa that morning were forgotten.

Mahesh traced a big fat zero in the sand with a long twig. He was sitting beside Nanju on one of the low stone benches that ringed the playground on three sides; a huge stone stage hogged the fourth end.

'But why would Armaan take it? He can't even write properly.' Mahesh gave Armaan, who was sitting in his wheelchair and soaking up the sun, a long, hard look.

Armaan's father was a seller of plastic pots and his mother worked as a domestic help. Making ends meet was a daily challenge in their family, and Armaan would often eat his first proper meal in school—at lunchtime. Every year Armaan grew a little smaller, a little weaker, and little less able to do the things he could do earlier.

'He's always asking for things. "Asha Miss, give socks." "Asha Miss, give book!"' Nanju answered with disgust. 'I'm sure it's him.'

Armaan's schoolbag contained a pencil, an old notebook that was filled with addition sums—Armaan loved numbers—and an extra pair of pants in case he soiled his school shorts. The bag hung from Armaan's wheelchair, its zip broken, the mouth open wide to receive anything anyone might care to pass onto its owner.

'Out!' someone screamed and everyone looked up.

Kevin was running around and waving his arms in front of the umpire.

'No!' the umpire shook his head. 'And stop wasting time!'

'It could also be Sangeetha,' Mahesh returned to the discussion, swinging his matchstick legs back and forth as he thought the matter through. 'She's always fighting with Aradhana.'

Sangeetha had joined United the previous year. She was used to topping the class in her former school. She was hearing impaired but she could lip-read and was also a sign-language whiz. And she was clearly determined to give Little Miss Perfect (as she called Aradhana) a run for her money.

'Yes, she's so jealous,' Nanju agreed, screwing up his forehead in distaste. 'It must be her only!'

'Or it could be Bhavani Amma.' Mahesh seemed determined to confuse Nanju.

As if on cue, Bhavani Amma walked past them, pushing the wheelchair of a small boy wearing a strained expression on his face. She was muttering under her breath about how one couldn't sit down for five minutes without someone or the other wanting to go to the toilet.

Bhavani Amma was notorious for making the wheelchair kids rot outside the bathroom for many long minutes before she deigned to take them in—by which time many of them had already done whatever it is they were waiting to do, in their wheelchairs. This invariably brought on a fresh stream of verbal abuse and humiliation. And so the children were careful around her.

'Why her?' Nanju asked, once she was safely out of earshot.

'She hates Aradhana,' Mahesh explained. 'Remember Aradhana's father complained about Karthik Uncle to Principal? And Principal shouted at him?'

Karthik Uncle was the driver of one of the school vans. He was known for his temper and the long, thin cane that he kept under his seat.

He had recently stopped the van halfway on the journey home and ordered Aradhana off; he said her nonstop chatter had given him a headache. No one knew the reason for this show of wrath. Nanju had heard some of the Ayammas talk about how Karthik Uncle had approached Aradhana's father, who was Someone Important in the Department of Sewage and Sanitation, for a handout and had been flatly refused. That could be the reason that Karthik Uncle picked on Aradhana all the time.

Aradhana had not planned to report the incident to her parents (no one crossed Karthik Uncle and lived). But one of her neighbours had seen her walking back home, and in spite of her protests, Aradhana's parents had reported the matter to the principal. Karthik Uncle had been told off and—even worse—he had had to apologise to the little girl. He had left her alone since, but everyone knew it was just the lull before the storm.

And everyone in the school knew that Bhavani Amma was Karthik Uncle's good friend. She was very diligent about cleaning the area where Karthik Uncle parked his van, all the while laughing and joking about something. This was also one reason why she was always late for toilet duty.

'But what will she do with Aradhana's notebooks?' Nanju never doubted Mahesh's genius, but he couldn't see how Bhavani Amma or Karthik Uncle could find any real use for Aradhana's notes.

'I don't know. But she can pick up the books any time she wants—the Ayammas are always in and out of the classrooms. And if the plan is to get Aradhana into trouble, then it's working perfectly.'

Aradhana had just about managed to hang on to her number one position in the unit tests that week—the results had been announced that morning—though, for the first time, Sangeetha had trumped her in Hindi.

'Help me, Nanju.' Mahesh wanted to get back into his wheelchair and as Nanju helped him, he spotted Aradhana walk up to a bench to join her friends.

Aradhana's thin face looked strained and the red-ribboned pigtails that constantly bobbed around—Aradhana was also the class chatterbox—hung glumly over each ear.

Theresa Miss had given Aradhana another tongue-lashing for being careless with her books. Theresa Miss was a stickler for neat and tidy work, and the children were expected to keep their books in immaculate condition—they weren't even allowed to write their names inside their books.

'That is why you have labels!' she had told the class on the first day of the school year. 'There's no need to keep writing your name all over the place. I don't need to constantly be reminded that it's your book I'm correcting!'

Nanju watched as Aradhana shifted her bag off her shoulders and sat down. Aradhana couldn't carry weight for very long as her back caved in and extended itself into her chest in the form of a gentle hump. This also left her legs a little uneven, and her right hip jutted upwards ever so slightly.

Aradhana opened her bag, and began to rifle through it. Everything seemed to be in order and so she zipped the bag close, cupped her face in her palms and stared straight ahead. A small sigh escaped her lips.

Nanju knew why Aradhana was so low. He had watched her a little while earlier when she had tried out for the sack race and had fallen twice. She had done this in spite of the teacher gently suggesting that she try out for something else as the sack race required some serious amount of thumping around.

'I know what we can do,' Nanju turned to Mahesh, a new resolve growing in his heart that would have given Jack's beanstalk a run for its money. 'We can keep an eye on them! I'll try and get something out of Bhavani Amma and Sangeetha. And Mahesh, you watch Armaan. How difficult can it be to catch the thief?'

'Go Kevin!' Asha Miss shouted from the other end of the playground.

The match wasn't going well.

The captain had hit a six and Nethra now needed six runs off four balls.

Kevin bit his lip and came back to bowl again.

Nethra hit two runs on the next two balls. All that was required were four more runs off the last two balls.

'Ronit! Stand there!' Pratik was brought forward and Ronit was dispatched to the back.

Even with one good arm, Ronit was a better fielder than Pratik.

A few more permutations and combinations were attempted before the umpire stepped in and threatened to give the match to Nethra if Kevin didn't stop wasting everyone's time.

Kevin ran up and bowled.

The batsman hit the ball hard and ran. He took one run, a determined look on his face.

A restless energy filled the air: Nethra needed two runs off the last ball to win the match.

Kevin waved his arms around one last time, and his small band of warriors, who were looking like they were all standing at the Mouth of Death, braced themselves for the last ball.

He ran up to the pitch and bowled.

The batsman swung his bat in the air and it connected with a resounding thwack. The ball flew in the air, higher and higher, before it began its descent towards the furthermost part of the playground.

This was where Ronit stood.

Ronit screwed up his eyes as he tried to follow the trajectory of the small brown sphere that was hurtling towards him like a deadly meteor.

Ronit's left arm was raised to the sky; the finger of god, that would make or break the match.

At last, the ball fell towards the earth, and Ronit caught it in one swift move, before it hit the ground.

'Yes!' Kevin pumped the air with his fist and did three perfect cartwheels as the playground erupted into happy mayhem.

Ronit was no longer visible; his small form was hidden under a pile of other small bodies that had thrown themselves on top of him.

At last, they had won.

Friday, 25 July

Thirty heads shot up at the word 'picnic'.

'When, Miss?'

'Wah! Picnic, Miss?'

'Tell, Miss, where?'

'Quiet!' was the answer they got, 'and those who don't finish their work won't be going!'

Asha Miss came into the classroom while everyone was still clamouring.

'Stand up and wish Miss! What bad manners this class has!' Theresa Miss glared at the students.

'Good morning, Miss!' Standard Five dutifully chanted in loud singsong voices.

'Good morning, children,' Asha Miss smiled.

'And Pratik! Look up! Show Miss your face,' Theresa Miss scowled at Pratik.

Pratik sat with his head bent low over his books. He had been in school for over a month now and was as distracted and naughty as when he had joined, though he had done surprisingly well in the unit tests. He stood up and gave Asha Miss a weak smile. There was something different about him; Nanju couldn't quite put his finger on it.

Theresa Miss solved the mystery: 'See, Miss! He's shaved off his eyebrows! And if you ask him, he won't say why.'

'When did this happen?' Asha Miss asked. She seemed to be trying to suppress a smile.

'This morning, I believe. Come here, Pratik!' Theresa Miss shouted and Pratik dragged his feet to her desk.

'At least tell Asha Miss why you did it!'

'No, Miss ...' Pratik whined, shaking his round face, which looked even rounder now thanks to the patchy smear of grey where his eyebrows used to be. 'I didn't do, Miss ...'

'What, no, Miss! Has your mother seen what you've done?'

'Yes, Miss ...'

'And your father?' Teresa Miss turned to Asha Miss before Pratik could answer. 'His father takes so much interest! Called me just the other day to check if the boy was completing all his work—and now look at this fellow!'

She turned back to Pratik: 'What did he say?'

'My Daddy out of station, Miss ... for full week.'

Even though Nanju was concentrating very hard—he was determined to carve out the sharpest possible point for his pencil with Mahesh's new blade—he allowed himself to be distracted for a moment: how he wished his Appa could also go out of station for a full week!

After the fiasco with the spelling test paper, Appa had been checking his bag regularly. Nanju had had to be extra vigilant and had disposed of all incriminating evidence at the earliest.

Appa would have been proud of Nanju's ingenuity if he could only have appreciated the amount of trouble it took to get rid of a stupid one-page answer sheet. One had to creep about and find a witness-free spot and even then it was essential to destroy all linkages, like one's name, before committing the act. The unit test answer sheets had been flushed down the toilet, thrown out of the van, or simply torn into shreds and dumped in the class dustbin.

Asha Miss asked Pratik about a perfectly formed oval scab that was peeling off Pratik's right arm, exposing a layer of fresh pink skin underneath.

'Hurt, Miss,' he explained.

'Hurt, Miss! Must have been fighting again, what else? Now go and sit down,' Theresa Miss dismissed him and informed Asha Miss that the picnic was on the following Friday.

'Principal decided that we must go somewhere educational,' said Theresa Miss, trying hard not to look too pleased. 'No neighbourhood parks. We will be visiting the Vigneshwara Science & Technology Park.'

Asha Miss did not seem as excited. 'Are you sure, Theresa Miss? Are they old enough to appreciate it?'

Nanju thought Theresa Miss seemed a bit disappointed at this response. 'Of course they are! And the park has a very nice endangered animals exhibit—I read all about it in the newspaper. They will enjoy.' Theresa Miss looked grumpier than before.

'Today's my birthday, Miss,' Ronit stood up as Asha Miss headed for the door, and the others went back to work, grumbling about how mean Theresa Miss was.

Ronit looked exceedingly smart. He was dressed in a black-and-white checked shirt and black trousers and his short black fringe fell in a neat line on his forehead. He brought out a box of toffees from his bag, walked up to Asha Miss, and pressed two shiny Nuttiness Coffee Creams into her hand.

'Happy birthday, Ronit,' Asha Miss stuck out her right hand.

Ronit's face changed. Asha Miss's face changed too—she looked like she'd been struck by lightning. She seemed to be debating whether she should drop her right hand and offer him her left one instead, but she continued to hold her right hand out.

Ronit shifted the box of toffees into a more comfortable position. Slowly, with visible effort, he raised his lifeless right arm and placed it into hers. She shook his hand gently and he let it fall back to his side.

'Thank you, Ronit. I will give these to my landlady's children,' Asha Miss said, in an extra-cheery voice.

'You eat, Miss!' The old Ronit was back to dismiss this silly idea.

Armaan whispered to Asha Miss to intercede for another toffee. But Ronit had already shoved the box back into the deepest corner of his bag and had a non-negotiable look on his face.

'Show-off!' Nanju muttered, slyly sucking on the toffee Ronit had distributed to the class a few minutes earlier. He too had begged for an extra toffee and his request had met with a similar reaction.

Then he heard the magic words.

'Nanjegowda, come for therapy—it's Friday.' The therapist called out from the doorway, and hurried off to round up students from across the school with motor skills similar to Nanju's.

Nanju enjoyed doing the exercises that were meant to strengthen his muscles and improve his coordination. He cheered up at the thought of heading out into the sunshine for a half-hour of much-needed respite.

For the week had been another long and boring one.

He had spent a lot of time agonising over his act for the Talent Show and had finally decided to bunk the whole affair.

'The Talent Show is really tensioning Miss,' he had confided to Asha Miss. 'Some are coming as Spiderman, some as something else, and I'm thinking, what to wear, what to wear. So best I don't come!'

They hadn't made any progress with the missing notebooks either. No notebooks had disappeared that entire week, and the investigation had come to a dead end.

Mahesh had been able to report back with some concrete information. He had made sure that his wheelchair had been parked close to Armaan at all times. He was happy to report—for Mahesh was rather fond of the gentle, soft-spoken boy—that Armaan was definitely not the culprit. Armaan simply wasn't strong enough to carry out the 'robberies'. He couldn't move without assistance and his hands had just enough strength to wield a pencil, and that too painstakingly.

Nanju had nothing useful to report, except that Sangeetha and Aradhana were not on talking terms. Aradhana had refused to share a computer with Sangeetha during computer class after she claimed she had seen a big black bug emerge from Sangeetha's mane and cut a track down her neck.

His interrogation of Bhavani Amma had also resulted in zilch.

'Go from here!' Bhavani Amma had ordered him when he'd hung back after lunch break and tried to chat her up as she swabbed the corridor.

Then he'd spotted her laughing and talking with Karthik Uncle on Tuesday afternoon. They were leaning against the van and Karthik Uncle's slim shoulders shook with laughter at something Bhavani Amma was saying.

Nanju thought Bhavani Amma would have made a formidable wrestler. She had broad muscular shoulders and walked with powerful strides. One could easily imagine her, as she squatted slightly in her colourful nylon sarees, slapping her thighs and readying herself for the onslaught.

Most of the kids were terrified of her. Her annoying whiny son—a skinny creature with a running nose in Standard Two—didn't make it any better. As a more senior member of the school, Nanju liked to give the young 'un a friendly tap on the head every now and then. Instead of feeling grateful at this display of affection, the little creep had complained about Nanju to his mother, and Nanju had got a hard rap on his own head and a warning to stay away from the boy.

Nanju had watched Bhavani Amma box Karthik Uncle playfully on the arm. He had been tempted to sidle up to them and try to listen in. But one look at Karthik Uncle's reptilian eyes had made him think better of it.

Yesterday, he had made one last attempt.

He had been on his way to the toilet and had spied Bhavani Amma sitting cross-legged in a corner of the courtyard, eating a small mountain of sambar rice from a big steel thali.

'Bhavani Amma ...'

'What?'

'Have you seen Aradhana?'

'No.'

Bhavani Amma continued to eat. Nanju tried again.

'Bhavani Amma ...'

'What?'

'Nothing ... just ...'

'WHAT?'

'Nothing! Nothing.'

And that had been the end of that.

'Hi Nanju.' Asha Miss fell in step with Nanju as he hurried to the Therapy Centre. Nanju walked with a sideways motion and he looked a little like the pendulum of a broken clock that swung violently from side to side. 'Where are you off to?'

'Therapy, Miss.'

The Therapy Centre was part of the school campus and a two-minute walk from the classrooms.

'I'm going in that direction too. Let's walk together.'

A pink flowering creeper grew alongside the path. It hummed with life as greedy nectar-sucking insects flew in and out of its broad green leaves. Shady jamun and mango trees lined the other side and the path led past a small nursery that was part of the school campus—though it also sold plants to the public—and was an oasis of calm in the otherwise chaotic school.

Nanju suggested they cut across the nursery.

The children were banned from entering it unless they were with a teacher, and Nanju was not about to let go of this opportunity to explore his favourite part of the school campus. The world's most wonderful job had to be that of the gardener, Ramappa, who was Nanju's good friend.

Nanju liked to spend time watching Ramappa bending over his beloved crotons, coaxing them to put on a multi-coloured leafy performance; limping across to scold a recalcitrant rosebush refusing to bloom or mercilessly pruning a lush green ficus—'It will grow better now, Nanju'.

Sadly, Theresa Miss showed no sympathy for his desire to linger when he should be in class.

'See Miss, this plant is kothmere—coriander—and this one is pudina.' Nanju bent down and quickly nicked a mint leaf off its stem. He crushed it between his fingers and took a deep breath of the fragrance.

'Nice smell, Miss.' He offered up his fingers for Asha Miss to ratify it. She sniffed politely and agreed that it did smell nice.

'And this rose, Miss. And this geranium—my mother keeps in pot ... kept,' he corrected himself.

Nanju's mother had had a special gift for loving everything that came her way—listless jasmine creepers that refused to blossom, lame stray dogs that had been kicked out of their packs, the neighbourhood 'mental': a middle-aged lady who roamed the streets with flowers sticking out of her short unkempt hair, and occasionally stopped by for a tumbler of coffee and some murukku—and she had shared this love for the world with her son. Now Nanju tended to the small pink geraniums that had once known the touch of his mother's rough calloused hands, and remembered to put out a small saucer of milk every morning for the old black cat that was slowly losing its eyesight.

He was rattling on about the kind of soil needed to grow tomatoes—really juicy ones—when Asha Miss spotted two small figures emerging from the rosebushes and creeping towards the exit.

'Who are those two?' she asked Nanju, who spun around and ordered the fleeing pair to stop.

The boys ground to a halt, each with a small flowerpot in his hands.

'Ay, what you're doing, man?' Nanju demanded, and then continued in explanation, 'Zafar and Junaid, Miss. Best friends from Standard Two.'

'Hello, you two,' Asha Miss ruffled Zafar's coir-like mop, as they both dutifully ran up.

Zafar was a blotchy little fellow with a skin disorder that had left his eyes extremely sensitive to the sun. He used to walk around everywhere with his right arm raised to his eyes, which meant he could hardly see at all. Then, after a particularly nasty fall, the principal had fitted Zafar with a pair of sunglasses. He now sported a snazzy pair of red-and-silver-streaked shades whenever he went out in the daylight.

Junaid had no legs and had been scooting along on leather-encased knees.

'Where are you off to?' Asha Miss asked kindly.

'Class, Mizz,' Zafar replied.

'What's that you're carrying?' Nanju wasn't going to be fobbed off so easily.

'Got gift, Mizz,' Zafar addressed his answer to Asha Miss.

'From whom?' His interrogator refused to let up.

'From class party,' Zafar stuck his chubby chin into the air and looked Nanju in the eye. 'Teacher told to come and take pot.'

Nanju was silenced. United had tied up with a few companies to sponsor occasional events in school, at the end of which, usually, the children were given small mementos to take home.

'Now isn't that a good idea?' Asha Miss said. Seeing Nanju's puzzled look, she continued, 'That the gift they have given the students are pots purchased from our very own nursery.'

'Yes, Miss,' Nanju agreed.

And before any more could be said, the duo said their goodbyes–'Bye Mizz'–and hurried off.

'Did you think they were ... taking the pots without permission?' Asha Miss smiled at Nanju.

Nanju shook his head and said no, but for a few seconds he had secretly hoped that Zafar and Junaid were stealing the plants–nabbing them would have turned him into an instant hero.

Like Appa, who had risked his own safety to turn in a colleague who had stolen money from the manager's wallet. Appa had managed to wean the truth out of the thief over a drink at the local bar, and had at first tried to persuade the man to give back the money. But the man had refused and threatened Appa with dire consequences if he spoke up. Appa had spoken up all the same and the man had been fired.

'But what if he tries to hurt you now, Appa?' Shanti Akka had been worried, when Appa had told them the story the previous night.

But Appa said that all that a poor man had was his reputation, and that it was more valuable than anything else in this world.

'Everyone thought it was poor Shivappa—he was the last one to leave the boutique that evening. If I hadn't exposed the thief, everyone would have pinned it on the old man. And a lifetime of honesty and hard work would have gone down the drain.'

'But why should they blame Shivappa Uncle, Appa? No one had seen him take it,' Nanju piped up.

'Come here.' Appa caught sight of Nanju's earnest face and smiled; he gently pulled him close. 'Everyone would have assumed that Shivappa took it, simply because they couldn't find the real thief. But don't you worry; in the end, the truth always wins. Now I hope you're being honest and telling me the truth about your work at school?'

And Nanju nestled closer to Appa's warm chest and lied through his teeth about his scholarly achievements. They were not too far from the truth: his notes were more or less up to date, and he had finished his homework in class (copying from Mahesh's work, as always) and there had been no more tests, so there were no results to lie about.

And Appa had called him his 'golden boy' and Nanju's face had shone like a diamond.

Friday, 1 August

The Class Monitor sat at the back of the van with a pair of frayed headphones tucked into his ears, a Nike cap on his head, the swoosh facing backwards, and a half-litre bottle of Sprite in his hands. No one sat beside him: he was the undisputed King of the Back Seat.

The Class Monitor's father was a flower merchant in Gussel Market and he liked to indulge his older son whenever he could. The boy was also the proud owner of an acid-washed denim jacket with flashy football patches sewn all over the front, just one more little thing that set him apart, and above, the rest of the rabble.

But what was worst was that he had the best double-decker pencil box anyone had ever seen.

It was a blue box with a soft plastic cover that took the shape of your finger when you pressed down on it. The pixie-sized pug prints took a few moments to lift off and disappear into the cosmos. Power Rangers fought fierce battles on the supine blue sky, their swords glittering like diamonds. The inside of the box came equipped with new Natraj pencils, car-shaped erasers and an automatic sharpener that whirred to life at the flick of a button. The lower deck had a set of brand-new sketch pens all nestled together in a cosy fashion. A secret compartment popped out at the press of a button. One couldn't help but hate the boy.

But every once in a while, the Class Monitor donned a new avatar, thanks to his seven-year-old brother, who also studied in United. The brother had bones as fragile as eggshells. His last fracture had happened when he had turned over in his sleep. This brother was, however, also the acknowledged champion of wheelchair racing. The Class Monitor was often spotted chasing after him in the courtyard, clucking away like an anxious mother hen trying to round up a rogue chick.

'Talk in English!' Theresa Miss reminded Ronit and Pratik who were sitting in the rear half of the van beside Asha Miss, jabbering away to each other in Tamil. Pratik was showing off the new pair of sports shoes that his Daddy had bought him the previous evening.

Standard Four and Standard Five were off to the Vigneshwara Science & Technology Park for their annual picnic. Theresa Miss hoped to spend the day broadening their horizons.

Nanju was sitting with Mahesh up front, next to Babu, the school's other van driver, but Nanju's eyes were glued to Karthik Uncle's van. It had been leading the convoy right from the start. What made it unbearable was that occasionally some rude fellow on the last seat would turn around and stick his tongue out at them.

Mahesh seemed unperturbed. Since he couldn't hold his head up for very long and it lolled back against the seat, he didn't care too much about what was happening outside.

But Nanju's blood boiled. If only Babu Uncle could drive a little faster, he thought. A quick glance at the big, dark man in the driver's seat showed that the chances of this happening were slim. Babu Uncle, a man of few words, and even less action, continued to drive the van with a complete lack of feeling: honking here, slowing down there, drumming lightly on the steering wheel and staring into space at the traffic lights. All this confirmed the sinking feeling in Nanju's heart that they were going to lose the race. He decided to think about something else.

'Mahesh, do you really think Sangeetha did it?'

'Maybe,' Mahesh answered, his head resting against the spongy rexine seat.

'But do you think she would have actually ...'

Nanju couldn't quite imagine the studious Sangeetha willfully ripping a book—any book—apart.

For the case of the disappearing and reappearing notebooks had been reopened.

Aradhana's English book had gone missing in the very first period on Monday, and had then turned up in Theresa Miss's desk just as they were leaving for the picnic.

Mahesh didn't answer immediately. But Nanju could tell he knew something that Nanju didn't.

The van finished navigating a stretch of road dotted with potholes that was sending shockwaves through Mahesh's spine. Now he could talk again.

'Aradhana's aiming for the school scholarship,' he informed Nanju. 'If she wins it, she gets 10,000 rupees.'

'She wants to join a coaching class with the money,' Mahesh went on. His mother knew Aradhana's mother and he had heard them discussing the matter. 'Her parents can't afford it—so if she wants to join the class, she must win the scholarship.'

United awarded cash scholarships to the toppers of Standard Five and Standard Six. The winners could use the money for anything educational, and Aradhana had set her heart on enrolling at the Bright Sparks Coaching Academy, as she badly wanted to join the Bright Sparks School after she finished with Standard 6 at United.

To win the scholarship, Aradhana needed to come first all three terms. And with some book or the other going missing every week, it was but inevitable that Aradhana would begin to fall behind—and Sangeetha pull ahead.

Evidently frustrated by the loss of her book for almost the entire week, Aradhana was looking for an opportunity to take on her competitor. What had started out as an argument in the last period the previous day, had suddenly escalated into a huge fight, with Aradhana eventually accusing Sangeetha of taking her books so as to sabotage her chances at the scholarship.

Sangeetha had made a couple of rude gestures in reply and had signed that she couldn't help it if Aradhana was dumb and couldn't cope! And it had all been very nasty and overwrought: a sobbing Aradhana was led by her sensitive cohort (there wasn't a dry eye in the group) to the toilet to cry her heart out, whilst the smaller, but equally outraged, rival faction stalked off to the playground with red faces that steamed indignation.

And then the book had been found the next morning—and in the teacher's own desk! A few pages had been ripped out from somewhere in the middle—someone had grabbed hold of the sheets and torn them out with deliberate malice. Nanju thought Sangeetha seemed most capable of such ferocity.

But as they were leaving for the picnic, Theresa Miss had decided to deal with it later. Also, Aradhana was absent. Her parents had called and pleaded a fever, though rumour had it that Aradhana had worked herself up into such a state after the fight the previous evening that she was on the verge of a 'nerves break'.

'Then let's watch Sangeetha!' Nanju said. 'It will be easier this time if we both keep an eye on her.'

Mahesh nodded. Then he closed his eyes and braced himself as the van hit a stretch lined with boulders.

Nanju went back to watching the road. He could just about spot Karthik Uncle's van ahead in the distance and it showed no signs of slowing down.

Theresa Miss's voice droned on in the background: she was telling Asha Miss another Pratik story.

'You know what this Pratik has been up to?'

Pratik promptly found something of great interest outside the window.

'Instead of going home in the van, he's been walking home for a week! If Karthik hadn't informed his parents on Monday that he hadn't been on the bus the previous week, nobody would have been any the wiser.'

'But why?'

'Because Karthik had shouted at him and threatened to stop taking him in the van—this fellow's always fighting with the other children—and so Mr Pratik decides on his own to stop using it!'

A cacophony of honking stopped all further conversation. The van fought for space under a newly constructed flyover, amongst the rush of vehicles that had come to a halt and the debris accumulated over the many years it had taken to build it.

'Really, Asha Miss,' Theresa Miss continued, as soon as they could hear themselves again, 'I don't know what to do with this Pratik. He's always disturbing the class—suddenly singing loudly or jumping around the place or dreaming about god knows what!'

'But he's clever.' Asha Miss had helped Theresa Miss out in class a few times and had been impressed with Pratik's work.

'Goes for tuitions! Father packs him off every day. But he's always making silly mistakes. And then absent constantly! Just this week he's bunked three days. If I hadn't called his mother last evening and insisted he come for the picnic, he'd have probably missed this as well.'

Theresa Miss glared at Pratik, who was still looking out of the window in a determined fashion.

'There's definitely something wrong with him ...' she muttered under her breath. 'I must talk to Principal.'

'Eat, Miss,' Ronit interrupted.

Ronit had come armed with a bagful of snacks: a packet of Kurkure, chocolate biscuits, a bottle of Mirinda. The Mirinda had been finished first. 'Not had breakfast, Miss' had been the explanation.

'How much longer?' Theresa Miss muttered, accepting a chocolate biscuit and looking at the shabby black watch that encircled her thin wrist.

She had hoped to reach the park by eleven, but it was already eleven thirty and they had been on the road for an hour and a half.

'Yay!' An excited yelp exploded from the front of the van as one of the children spotted Karthik Uncle's van stuck ahead of them at a signal. Karthik Uncle's van had been missing for some time now and everyone had accepted defeat.

But now Babu Uncle slowly inched forward, and the kids began to cheer and holler as their van passed Karthik Uncle's, now honking away at a bike that had broken down in front of it.

Thirty small thumbs immediately began to stab downwards in mid-air; the losers responded by sticking out pink tongues and making monkey faces.

But within minutes, they were stuck at a signal and Karthik Uncle's van was spotted pulling ahead and taking a turn.

A loud groan erupted.

'Quiet!' The usually impassive Babu Uncle shouted, and everyone held their breath and watched the road, especially the crossroads. One could never tell where Karthik Uncle might emerge from; the race was not over yet.

Then, after what seemed like an eternity, they took the last turn, and there was the other van, still ahead.

And so, the indefatigable Karthik Uncle won again.

Both vehicles pulled in to the big parking lot of the science park, and everyone clambered out, and claimed to have come first.

'Miss, where's toilet, Miss?' Nanju bobbed up and down to get Theresa Miss's attention.

But Theresa Miss was busy arguing with the class teacher of Standard Four.

'At least they can play on the swings and slides there, Theresa Miss!'

The class teacher of Standard Four, who had joined Standard Five on their picnic, was proposing that they turn right round and go all the way back to Brutchins Park, a popular public park that was a stone's throw away from school. For there was no getting away from it: The Vigneshwara Science & Technology Park was a teeny tiny bit of a letdown.

The Park boasted a set of huge red and blue plastic structures that soared up to the sky, and might well have been rocket launchers for all the kids cared.

Ronit tried to lead a small band of brigands up the first few blue rungs, and was promptly hauled back by one fast-reddening ear.

'It's not for their age,' the stony-faced lady, who was escorting them around, constantly reminded Theresa Miss.

Then the kids were walked, pushed and carried up a flight of stairs to the 'Museum', a long tube-lit room that housed a few faded shells (a tag proudly proclaimed they were 'Ammonite Fossils') and a couple of lonely bleached corals that hid inside glass cupboards that stretched from floor to ceiling and lined the room on both sides.

'You should have told us about the wheelchairs,' the lady complained to Theresa Miss for the tenth time.

And then they were taken down more steps and came face to face with an enormous playground that had to be crossed to reach the promised land: the Endangered Animals Park.

Even Karthik Uncle had begun to feel sorry for the kids and decided to pitch in. He pushed Mahesh's wheelchair. Babu Uncle carried two of the smallest children on his shoulders. Asha Miss tried to get everyone to sing a song as they hobbled onwards, and Theresa Miss reminded everyone that they had saved the best for last. The Endangered Animals exhibit was the highlight of the park, and the children were going to love it.

At last, the crossing was made. Everyone slowly fell silent as their eyes took in the cheap and cheerful habitat of a bunch of animal statues painted bright fluorescent colours. Tigers and rhinos and giraffes and an elephant that had long white tusks but was about the same size as a zebra that it stood next to, and even a dinosaur—a grinning grey T-Rex—were lined up like a bunch of obedient school kids on the other side of a deep ditch. They were endangered enough to require protection even when created out of concrete.

'Miss, dinosaurs are also in danger, Miss?' one of the girls piped up, ever-eager to ask an intelligent question.

She was rewarded with an abrupt 'Don't talk rubbish!' This final exhibit was also finished with at top speed, and at last the little party collapsed onto pink and purple benches in a small patch of shady green and tried to catch their breath.

They were immediately informed that this was the nursery.

'Children break pots, madam,' a couple of sulky gardeners grumbled, as they stationed themselves around the area. There was to be no play here either.

And through it all Nanju kept an eye out for the toilet and hoped and prayed that his diaper would hold out.

Mahesh and one of the boys from Standard Four sat in their wheelchairs and threw a big plastic ball at each other.

With every throw, the boy gave three sharp whistles: 'Phee! Phee! Phee!'

Mahesh was his usual dignified self.

The children had been left to their own devices in the nursery, playing furtive games of hide-and-seek until the closest mali shouted at them to stop, or fighting over the free toys that came in chips packets purchased for the picnic, or pottering around for odds and ends that were free for the taking.

Ronit was determined to collect the highest number of gundulmanis, the oval red seeds that were great for flicking at the back of unsuspecting heads. Sadly, everyone else seemed to have the same idea.

'Psst, Pratik ...' Ronit hissed. 'Come this side.'

He waved in the direction of the Endangered Animals Park. It was a stone's throw from the nursery, and if they could slip off without anyone seeing them, was sure to be rich with unexplored treasures.

Pratik shook his head.

'Foot paining,' he said, sitting put on the bench and using his teeth to tear open the Mango Frooti tetrapack that Theresa Miss had just handed out.

Ronit turned away in disgust. Normally, Pratik could be counted on for a bit of fun, but today he was going on and on about his stupid feet and had even declined Ronit's offer to race across the playground earlier. 'Serves him right for showing off about his new shoes,' Ronit muttered.

He looked around. The teachers were getting ready to serve lunch that had been brought in three huge containers from school: vegetable pulav, raita and kesari bhath, a sweet sticky porridge studded with raisins. Ronit's tummy gave a low rumble.

Even the gardeners had thawed a little at the prospect of a hot meal and were bustling around Theresa Miss and the other teachers as they fussed over where to sit and how to dish out the food.

Then Asha Miss dropped the kesari bhath, and Ronit took his chance and slipped into the ditch. He clambered out and hid behind a small pink elephant with the long tusks and waited.

No one seemed to have noticed.

Theresa Miss was trying to convince a weepy Asha Miss that the kesari bhath wouldn't be missed all that much.

The class teacher of Standard Four (who was almost in tears herself—she was very fond of kesari bhath) was shooing away the inquisitive mob that had gathered to see what the commotion was all about.

The gardeners were muttering under their breath, as they tried to sweep the sticky goo off their organic grass.

And the van drivers quietly helped themselves to cups of tea from the big flask that they had lugged along with all the other dishes all the way from the parking lot to the nursery.

The coast was clear for exploring enough to fill the heart of any true-blue adventurer.

Ronit put his head down and went to work, ducking under the bellies of the zebra, the tiger and the rhino, and then getting down on his knees and looking under the T-Rex's tail.

It was there that he met Nanju.

Nanju had just finished a diaper change and was zipping up when Ronit's head popped up into the little pocket of space under the big reptilian tail.

A small patch of wet earth stood between Nanju's feet. Tucked away under the deepest part of the dinosaur's tail was a soiled diaper that announced its presence with the hint of a breath-stopping odour.

'Miss! Theresa Miss!' Ronit didn't think twice.

He leapt to his feet, scaled the ditch in one smooth jump, and ran up to announce his exciting new discovery.

Monday, 4 August

'Akka, I've got 100!' Nanju shouted across the room to Shanti Akka.

'Are you sure?' his sister shouted, continuing to shovel spoonfuls of curd rice into Nanju's plastic lunch box. She reached for the jar of pickle, dug out a small piece of lime, tossed it on top of the squidgy mix and clamped the box shut.

'Yes, come and check if you like.'

He limped over and pushed the thermometer into Shanti Akka's face: 'See—100!'

Nanju had woken with a series of complaints that morning—his head was hurting, his eyes were burning—and he insisted on walking around the room with a thin blanket wrapped around his shoulders, most of it trailing on the floor.

Shanti Akka and Appa had both touched his forehead and declared him to be fine.

'Hmm ... no, it's 98. You have to go to school, Nanju.'

'I'm not going, Akka! You hear me?'

'Don't let Appa hear you, that's all.'

Appa was in the bathroom.

'I don't care! Let Appa beat me also ... I'm still not going!'

As if on cue, Appa walked into the room and reached for his waist.

'Appa, I'm not going. My stomach is really paining.'

Nanju began to cry, both from terror of the angry red welts that the belt promised to burn into his thighs, and fear of what he would have to face in school after what had happened on Friday.

'Stop crying and come here.' His father's hand was in his trouser pocket from which he pulled out a small plastic box.

He opened it and a sleek black watch with a grey rim around the dial stared up at Nanju. On the dial was a menacing Batman, lunging forward to take off. Below this electrifying figure was a small panel that told the time in bold numbers: 7:15.

'Nice?' he asked as he strapped it onto his son's wrist.

Shanti Akka had told Appa about the picnic. Mahesh lived close by and she was friends with his sister.

'Leave it to me,' Appa had said, and sat down on his sewing machine and spent the whole of Sunday—his only day off—stitching an elaborate salwar kameez so that he might earn an extra three hundred rupees and buy Nanju the watch of his dreams.

Even though Appa's legs throbbed with a dull pain and his fingers were sore, he knew it had been worth it as his son's eyes grew wide and a big goofy smile lit up his face. Nanju forgot all about dirty diapers and wet spots and thought of just how jealous his classmates were going to be.

After his father had strapped on his new watch, there had been no choice but to get on the van, and for the first few minutes Nanju could hardly even look Mahesh in the face.

But as the chatter and din in the van indicated that everyone was busy minding their own business, Nanju slowly turned around and began to scrutinise his classmates.

He first noted that Aradhana was still absent, and he was disappointed. He would have loved to show her his new watch, and anyway, he had never expected any unkindness from her.

Sangeetha sat in what was usually Aradhana's place, signing away at full speed to her neighbour—something about a new dress that was green and blue and pink and gold.

'After taking her books, Sangeetha's taken Aradhana's place also!' Nanju couldn't help whisper to Mahesh, shocked at this bold display of aggression. Everybody knew Aradhana had the best seat in the van, not too far behind where the rowdier kids sat, nor too much up front near Karthik Uncle, but in the sweet spot right in the middle.

Mahesh craned his head for a look and nodded, suitably impressed.

Nanju then turned his attention to Pratik, who sat in his usual spot behind Aradhana—Sangeetha today—and was spitting bits of paper out of the window at innocent passers-by. He had been most worried about Pratik's reaction. Ronit wasn't in Nanju's van, but Pratik was Ronit's best friend and that was bad enough.

But even when Pratik had seen him, nothing had happened. Instead, Pratik had crinkled his eyes and shook his head, silently begging Nanju not to rat on him, for Nanju had the reputation of keeping Karthik Uncle informed about the goings-on at the back of the van.

And the morning had continued to remain good, and except for the one passing remark from Ronit as they walked into school together—'Wore your chaddi, eh?'—it might never have happened.

Nanju knew that this wasn't because Ronit had had a sudden change of heart—one look at Ronit's face told him just how much he was itching to bring up Nanju's recent past. He had overheard Theresa Miss warning Ronit to drop the subject or else she would complain to Principal about him.

Everyone in class knew that Ronit's operation was to be sponsored by the school and was scheduled for the end of September. There was hope that Ronit's arm might be set right. Getting into trouble with Principal now was not a smart thing to do. And if nothing else, Ronit was smart.

Asha Miss watched as the tea passed her by, as it had done every day since she had joined United School.

'Excuse me ...'

The Standard Five gang was watching the alphabet song on YouTube as it downloaded in fits and bursts on her phone. Asha Miss had decided to go back to the basics.

'E is for elefant ... eh-eh-elefant,' Ronit sang loudly.

Bhavani Amma ignored Asha Miss and strode past, thermos in one hand, small steel cups stacked together in a pyramid in the other. Bhavani Amma was in charge of making and distributing the tea, and all new assistant teachers learnt very quickly that she didn't believe it necessary to offer them a cup.

'Amma ...' Asha Miss tried again.

Bhavani Amma ignored her and walked into the administration office instead, dispensed a cup to each occupant, and swiftly set off across the courtyard. Asha Miss resigned herself to another tea-less day.

'Bhavani Amma! Miss want tea,' Mahesh shouted.

Bhavani Amma turned around.

'No tea!' she said, looking Asha Miss in the eye. 'Finished.'

Asha Miss turned her attention to Ronit.

'Not elefant, Ronit,' she said, trying to break the news to him gently. 'Elephant. Like the fin of a fish.'

'Elefant,' Ronit rhymed 'fant' with pant, twirling a silver band round and round his left thumb. He also sported a pinkish-blue plastic band on his middle finger that was tinted with the hues of the ocean.

'Cool band,' Asha Miss stopped to compliment him. 'And nice ring too!'

'He's become like a rowdy, Miss,' Mahesh said, displaying his marvellous white teeth in a 100-watt smile.

'E is for elefant ... eh-eh-elefant ...'

'No. Elephant. Let me play that again.'

'E is for elephant,' Ronit sang correctly.

'Yes, that's right.'

'But in Tamil we say elefant, Miss.'

'Hi, Miss,' Pratik ran up. He had been excused from class to watch over his baby sister Blessy, who was trailing along behind him in a short pink frilly frock whilst Theresa Miss talked to his mother.

Theresa Miss had called for an immediate meeting with his mother that morning when she arrived into class to find him kicking the Class Monitor in the ribs. He had refused to explain himself and had just stood there with his head bowed, though some of the children shouted out that the Class Monitor had started it, and had kept trying to touch the cut above Pratik's lip.

'Shaving again, eh?' Theresa Miss had shouted. The Class Monitor—to everyone's delight—had also been given a warning.

A wisp of hair held together by a glittering green rubber band stuck up like a fountain on the top of Blessy's head. A smudge of black kajal on her cheek guarded her from any possible evil eye.

Pratik was a proud brother. He stood back and watched fondly as Blessy toddled over to the stone table and amused everyone by spinning round and round till she fell to the ground in a messy heap, thereby exposing a pair of grey buttocks that sent them all off into giggles.

'How old is she, Pratik?'

'One and half, Miss.'

'And you?'

'Ten, Miss.'

'Wow. That really makes you a big brother to this naughty little girl, doesn't it?' Asha Miss reached out to tickle Blessy, who promptly ran to her brother and hid behind his legs, peering from between his knees every once in a while to see if it was safe to reappear.

'Yes, Miss,' Pratik laughed.

He was summoned by a visibly agitated Theresa Miss.

The class went back to singing.

Kevin strolled past. He was on one of his usual jaunts during class: sometimes to the toilet, sometimes for a drink of water, most times for a breath of fresh air.

He stopped and stared as Ronit sang in his best voice: 'F is for pish. Pish, Pish, Pish.'

Ronit caught him staring.

He faltered for a second; then continued to sing, staring straight ahead, his voice loud and determined.

Kevin's eyes narrowed as he watched Ronit. Then he waved to Asha Miss and walked off.

Asha Miss's little group started work on the number names.

'Why didn't you come to school last week, Mahesh?' Asha Miss asked, as Mahesh copied down 'TWENTY' in his notebook. No one else had progressed beyond ten.

'White blood low, Miss,' Mahesh answered cheerfully. He had been hospitalised for two days the previous week and had almost missed the picnic. 'Fine now, Miss.'

'Good, sweetheart.'

'Good, sweetheart ...' Ronit mimicked, under his breath.

'Shutyamouth!' Nanju butted in angrily. He had not forgiven Ronit for telling on him and he was itching to take him down a few pegs.

This was always more possible in Asha Miss's class.

'You shut your mouth!' Ronit retorted, and peering into Nanju's book, 'And you can't spell "three" also? Ha!'

'Miss! Always he laughs!' Nanju complained, his face growing hot.

'He who laughs last, laughs loudest,' Asha Miss smiled around the group. She was rewarded with blank looks.

'Do you know it's my birthday today?' she asked, and everyone shouted out 'Happy birthday, Miss!' Asha Miss fished in her purse for the bars of Dairy Milk that she had bought for them.

'Miss, you celebrate in big way, Miss?' Nanju asked, his eyes growing wistful as he sucked on his fast-disappearing bar of chocolate that had leaked onto his fingertips and turned them rusty.

'No, I'm a little big for all that now. What about you, Nanju?'

'Yes, Miss, I get big cake.'

'Wow! And when is your birthday?'

'Don't know, Miss.' He examined the wrapper as he tried to squeeze out the last hidden bits of brown velvet, and did not notice Miss Asha's look of surprise.

'Okay, let's finish up now. How do you spell four?' Asha Miss looked at the girl on her right.

The kids were marking off the correct answers in their books.

'F-O ... V-R!' was the confident reply.

'No. F-O-V-E!' Nanju corrected his classmate, thereby consolidating his position as the worst speller of the group.

Mahesh had got all twenty words correct. Ronit had rubbed out any misspelt words and quickly corrected them as the answers were been read out, so he too had a perfect score.

'Miss, game, Miss!'

Asha Miss looked at her watch; there were still five minutes to go.

'Okay, let's play the word game.'

The word game was a version of Antakshari, but instead of singing a song, they had to make a word with the last letter of the previous word.

Ronit wanted to go first. He had to find a word that started with R.

'Rat!' he shouted, voicing what many in the group thought of him.

It was Asha Miss's turn next. She had to come up with a word that started with T.

'To; like, I have to go to the bathroom,' and she pointed to the bathroom that was down a small alley.

Then Asha Miss realised that to also sounded like the number two, and because this fitted in so well with the number names that they had just practised, she decided to explain further.

'It also sounds like two, the number two, doesn't it?' she said, holding up two fingers.

Ronit sniggered and dug his neighbour in the ribs.

'No, I don't mean that ...'

Some more giggles broke out.

'I don't mean I want to go to the bathroom for Number Two ...' she rushed on.

But it was hopeless; the kids were in splits.

Only Nanju held back. He looked at Asha Miss and his eyes widened a little. They were filled with pity.

Nanju watched as Kevin soundlessly walked up to Ronit, who stood near the water cooler in a quiet corner of the courtyard.

It was snack break. Nanju and Mahesh were sitting on their usual bench eating their tiffin. Ronit had swung by for a drink of water before heading back to rejoin Pratik in the playground.

Ronit finished, and swung around to find Kevin, three inches away and at least a foot taller, towering over him.

Kevin said nothing; his eyes were locked onto Ronit's.

Then he bumped Ronit's knees with his own and the smaller boy's knees instantly buckled. Kevin bumped him again and again. Ronit's small face shrank further as he kept straightening up after every hard knock. He was also trying very hard to hold back the tears that were welling up at the corners of his eyes.

'Kevin! Leave!' the old Ayamma shouted.

She had spotted them on her way to the school hall where all the teachers and Ayammas had decided to gather during the snack break to wish the highly popular Asha Miss for her birthday.

Kevin gave Ronit one last look and took a step back. Then he turned and walked away.

'Rombo panrey ne! You're acting up too much nowadays!' the Ayamma shouted after him. 'Go, ma.' She patted Ronit kindly on the head and hurried off as fast as her old legs would allow.

Ronit made his way to the bathroom to wash his wet face.

Nanju knew Ronit was paying the price for standing up to Kevin earlier. He should have just stopped singing, Nanju thought, instead of trying to act like a hero. Kevin was not one to take a snub lightly.

Ronit walked past Nanju and Mahesh, and shot them a quick look as if he was bracing himself for what was to come.

Nothing did, and Ronit passed by in a surprisingly shared and comforting silence.

Like many disabled people, Nanju and Mahesh were often at the receiving end of endless bullying and teasing. When most people first saw Mahesh—with his oversized head and pint-sized body—they tended to shrink back in horror. And Nanju, with his sideways pendulum walk and simple open face, never failed to evoke a laugh. Nanju and Mahesh both knew exactly how tall Ronit was feeling at the moment.

'But then who did it, Nanju?' Mahesh returned to their conversation.

Another book had gone missing that morning, after they had returned from their session with Asha Miss. But this time it had been Sangeetha's science book.

'How do I know?' Nanju mumbled, looking down and fiddling with the clamps of his tiffin box.

They had lost their prime suspect in one fell swoop. What was worse, Nanju had a bad feeling that Sangeetha thought it was him!

And all because he had tried to copy a few lines from her stupid science book last Thursday when Mahesh had been absent. She had got all cross and threatened to report him to Theresa Miss if he didn't stop.

After her book had gone missing this morning, Sangeetha had been giving him dirty looks all through the last period before snack break. When the bell rang, and he had run to grab a wheelchair for Mahesh—before all the good ones were taken—Nanju had seen her whispering something to her friends, and they had turned and given him a strange look. How Nanju wished he had stuck to his guns and stayed at home. Even his Batman watch didn't make him feel any better.

Mahesh ignored this unusual response and instead pulled out a piece of paper from his pocket. On it was a calendar that he had copied from his school diary after finishing his classwork. He had decided to work more scientifically, like the detectives in his favourite Kannada serial *Karnataka Kriminals*, and had noted down all the details of the case.

July 2014

Sun	Mon	Tue	Wed	Thurs	Fri	Sat
		1	2	3	4	5
6	7 A's science book found on wheelchair	8	9	10 A's maths book goes missing	11	12
13	14	15	16	17	18 A's maths book found in dustbin. ← Cricket match	19 Suspects: Annaan, Sangeetha, Bhavani Anna & kavthik Uncle. Motive: hate Aradhana
20	21	22	23	24 No books missing this week	25	26
		Suspects: Annaan off the list as cannot commit such a crime				
27	28 A's English book goes missing	29	30	31 A & S fight		

August 2014

Sun	Mon	Tue	Wed	Thurs	Fri	Sat
					1 picnic	2
3	4	5	6	7	8	9
10	11	12	13	14	15	16
17	18	19	20	21	22	23
24	25	26	27	28	29	30
31						

5/6 English book missing
Key suspects: ???
Motive: ???

A's English book found in Theresa Miss's desk — pages ripped
Key suspects: Sangeetha, but B
Amnark Uncle still on list

'See man, Nanju,' Mahesh shoved the calendar under Nanju's nose.

Nanju reluctantly looked over and blanched at the last entry.

Mahesh had decided to knock Bhavani Amma and Karthik Uncle off the suspect list, as they had nothing against Sangeetha. Of course, Sangeetha herself was off the hook as well. So who had done it?

'Don't know ...' Nanju managed to spit out, his favourite onion uttapam turning to sawdust in his mouth.

'But I know,' someone spoke up. 'It's Kevin.'

Ronit hurried on, as Nanju and Mahesh turned to him in surprise.

'He lives near my house, and he's been boasting to everyone that he's been up to something "special" in school. Then one of the older boys made fun of him the other day, and Kevin got really angry and told them to wait till Friday. He said he was going to do something very big this Friday.'

'Just because he roughed you up, don't blame him, okay?' Nanju glared at Ronit.

Then Nanju's heart beat a little faster when he realised the consequences of this revelation. He would be off the hook! But how would they prove this wild theory? And that too proposed by an untrustworthy skunk like Ronit!

'And why would he want to take anyone's books?' Mahesh agreed, putting his Criminal Calendar, as he liked to think of it, back into his pocket.

'He's trying really hard to impress the older boys in the slum—wants to be included in all their gangster stuff, I guess,' Ronit continued patiently. 'It's all just a game for him ... just to prove how he can get away with anything. And as he's always roaming around school—it wouldn't be difficult for him to dart into class and make off with something.'

Mahesh wanted to ask Ronit how he had figured out what they were talking about, but he said nothing. Ronit might have his uses.

'I can help you if you want ...'

It was a stunning offer. Ronit, who liked nothing better than to tease and torment and bully, was actually offering to help.

At any other time, Nanju would have shouted out a loud impassioned 'No!' After all, Ronit was his Number One Nemesis. But desperate times called for desperate measures and he bit back the words.

Mahesh spoke up. 'Okay. But how?'

'I'll try and keep an eye on him this week ...'

'And what's he going to do on Friday?' Nanju demanded.

But Ronit only shrugged; he didn't know anything more.

'Friday is the Talent Show,' Mahesh answered, speaking slowly, as his brain whirred at top speed. 'He must be planning a bigger haul. First Aradhana, then Sangeetha, now maybe one book from every bag. Who knows what Kevin might do?'

'But how will we catch him?' Nanju asked, cracking all ten knuckles of his fingers, and then trying again. 'All the kids have to be in the hall! Either participating or watching.'

Silence fell over the little group as they pondered the might of their new adversary.

This wasn't any ordinary boy: this was Kevin.

'Maybe ... I could hide in the big cane basket that's kept at the back of the classroom, the one that was used to store the balls and bats. It's empty now.' Mahesh sat up a little harder than usual at this exciting idea. Since he couldn't sit up without needing to throw himself forward, he almost hit the stone bench in front of him. He righted himself and continued. 'I'll pretend I'm not feeling well and want to rest in class, and you can put me into the basket before you leave for the hall. I'll be able to see quite clearly through its holes.'

'Suppose he sees you?' Nanju didn't like the idea of leaving Mahesh alone with Kevin in the empty classroom. He wished he could be the one hiding, but he knew he lacked the courage.

'He'll never dream I'm in that old basket!' Mahesh grinned. 'And once he's gone, I'll topple the basket over, crawl to the hall and tell Theresa Miss everything. She'll only have to check his bag to know the truth.'

Mahesh was a favourite of Theresa Miss's and so this part seemed plausible.

Ronit said nothing, but he looked at Mahesh with a new respect. And though Nanju still worried for Mahesh's safety, his eyes gleamed with hope. If anyone in the world could pull this off (and save him!), it was his best friend.

'There's no other way.' Mahesh closed the subject and opened his tiffin box in his usual calm manner. He surveyed its contents: two fluffy white idlis and a dollop of mint-green chutney, and his stomach gave a happy rumble. 'Don't worry. I'll be all right.'

Friday, 8 August

Kevin shifted from foot to foot as he waited for his cue. He didn't have to wait long. The tempo changed almost immediately, the drums pounding out an irresistible beat.

He strode forward, whipped off the blue polyester sleeveless jacket that he was wearing over his white shirt, and tossed it over his shoulder.

The four girls from Standard Six who flanked him, two to a side, did some elaborate pirouettes as he narrowed his eyes and glowered at the gaping audience seated at his feet, the shoulder with the jacket stuck out at a sharp right angle.

Then the music changed.

'Why this Kolaveri Kolaveri Kolaveri di?' filled the hall and a loud cheer went up.

The music had an unhurried lazy rhythm and Kevin moved his body with a casual grace and fluidity—hipping and hopping, hot stepping and break dancing. The girls struck dramatic poses on either side of the stage as the star of the show, radiating cool from every pore of his body, danced on.

The audience clapped and cheered and hooted (the teachers' faces had turned to stone), and then, all too soon, the music stopped.

Kevin turned on his heel and strode off, the girls trailing behind like the twinkling tail of a comet, and to the cheering and adulation of the fans.

'Wow, Kevin anna!'

'Kevin na, supaar!'

'Super, Kevin na!'

Kevin shot a quick look at Asha Miss and was rewarded with a big thumbs-up. He acknowledged this with an abrupt nod and stepped out into the corridor.

Nanju watched him leave and his heart began to beat an exciting little tempo of its own. Would Kevin do the 'big thing' he had boasted about to his pals? Nanju crossed his fingers and hoped for a miracle.

The teachers sat lined up against the walls of the big hall, and the principal sat at a small table right in front of the stage along with a visiting dignitary, in the role of the judges.

Theresa Miss sat beside Asha Miss and tried to look pleasant, but her mouth kept drooping off at the sides whenever she lost focus, and she soon gave up.

'What is Standard Five doing?' Asha Miss whispered.

At the Talent Show, prizes were awarded for the Best Class Performance, the Best Individual Performance and the Best Costume, and the class teacher of the winning class always got a lot of importance.

'Nothing! No parents take interest,' Theresa Miss shook her head dejectedly.

'Oh, did you call for them? I would have liked to meet some of the parents,' Asha Miss replied.

'Didn't call ... but they can also come, no?' Theresa Miss threw the ball firmly back into the parents' court.

Except for the Class Monitor's speech about the 'Nine Golden Commandments of Being a Good Citizen' that Theresa Miss had forced him to learn the previous day, and Aradhana's speech about teachers, which Aradhana had written herself, the flag of Standard Five was definitely flying at half-mast.

Nanju sat somewhere in the middle of the audience seated on the ground, while those in wheelchairs commanded the best seats right at the back of the room. He was more excited than he could ever remember being.

It had been a long hard week for him, a suspect on the run. Every time he saw Sangeetha anywhere, he had taken to his crooked heels and disappeared around the nearest corner.

Sangeetha used to sit in the row immediately behind him, but now had moved three rows away—probably to keep her precious books safe, Nanju thought bitterly. A few of the other girls had also begun to look at him as if he were some kind of poisonous insect that needed to be exterminated at the earliest. This number, mercifully, did not include Aradhana.

But Nanju did not know whether this was because she didn't believe Nanju capable of such stealth and trickery or because the cold war between the girls still continued. Aradhana had been forced to accept that Sangeetha wasn't the thief. But because Sangeetha was rumoured to have said that Aradhana's hair was like a rat's tail, passions still ran high.

Sangeetha's book had turned up on Wednesday, tossed on to the floor at the back of the classroom and smelling of old potato peel. But this had not changed things for Nanju. After all, the accusing eyes seemed to say, who knows when this mad fellow will strike next?

Nanju's greatest fear was that Sangeetha would get it into her stuffy head to inform Theresa Miss of her suspicions. Then he was well and truly a goner.

For Nanju had to admit: he was the perfect suspect.

He had the motive: he sucked in studies, and moreover, there was that little issue of being branded the class copycat. He was present at the scene of the crime: he just needed to lean back to nick the book. And he had no alibi either: Mahesh had been absent that fateful day and no one else could be counted on to support him.

As he looked around the hall, he was happy to see that Sangeetha and her coterie were sitting all the way down the line. Now that he had bigger problems to deal with, Nanju thought how silly he'd been to ever dread the Talent Show.

Except for Mahesh, keeping watch in the dusty cane basket, everyone else was in the hall. Ronit and Pratik were sitting near him; they, too, weren't participating in anything.

They had had the chance to test Ronit's theory on Wednesday. Kevin had dropped by at their mid-morning session with Asha Miss and had insisted on joining in one round of 'Name, Place, Animal, Thing'.

'Miss, do all countries punish people who rob things?' Mahesh had suddenly piped up.

He had finished writing down a word in each category that started with J—Jayprakash, jungle, jackal and jug—and took his chance to try and smoke out the rat.

'Yes, of course. Stealing is a crime anywhere. Why, Mahesh?'

'Nothing, Miss, simply.'

Mahesh, however, had got his answer.

Kevin had looked up with a start on hearing the question and had given Asha Miss a distinctly furtive look. And he had left abruptly—'Bye Miss, teacher calling', something that had never bothered him in the past. He ran off with Pratik, who was passing by after a recent excursion to the toilet.

Sangeetha's missing book had turned up soon after this conversation. Just after lunch break, it was found lying on the floor at the back of the room, beside the window that overlooked the corridor. Kevin could have simply tossed it in as he passed by. Though, thought Nanju, Sangeetha and gang thought he had thrown it there.

Nanju hadn't breathed a word about this new turn of events to Mahesh, but Nanju knew Mahesh knew. Nothing much happened in school, let alone their class, without Mahesh hearing about it. But Mahesh hadn't said a word either. Nanju had never felt more grateful for his friendship.

Today would be the day they would catch the culprit red-handed. And Mahesh, hot and sweaty with an itchy nose—there really was a lot of dust in the basket—and Nanju, marooned on an island of fear and desperation amongst the boisterous hordes, couldn't wait for the moment to arrive.

'Teachers teach us good things. We respect our teachers. Our teachers are like our gods.'

Aradhana, dressed as Barbie, was giving a solemn speech.

The teachers beamed; Nanju's mouth dropped open.

Aradhana looked radiant. Her mother had plaited her fine soft hair and tied it back in a loose bun that was held in place by a shiny gold clip. Her lips were the colour of cotton candy and her cheeks were tinted with rouge. A frilly frock fell in flouncy waves around her thin twisted body. 'Barbie' was painted onto a pink satin sash that she wore over her right shoulder. The shiny red circles of tinsel paper that were sewn all over her dress glittered in the sunlight like fiery planets.

'Thank you teachers for all your teaching. Have a good day.'

Aradhana left the stage to thunderous applause.

A boy in a wheelchair, wearing an elephant suit, was up next.

Meanwhile, the audience was entertaining itself. There was plenty to see among the participants of the Fancy Dress.

At the back of the room, among the rest of the wheelchair crowd, was Grape Boy, according to a piece of paper stuck on one of his balloons. Green balloons were plastered all over his green shirt and shorts. Fat juicy balloons covered his face and head—only a pair of chubby cheeks and two happy brown eyes could be seen.

Grape Boy giggled as a friend leaned over and began to burst the green balloons. His father, in his auto driver's uniform, was not amused. It had taken him an hour to blow up all the balloons. He frowned and moved the wheelchair just out of reach.

Many parents had accompanied their wards to school that day, thrilled to see their children shine in the spotlight.

Bottle Boy had empty plastic bottles hanging off every possible part of him and his wheelchair, and Milk Boy tottered around on his walker, smothered in washed and dried-out milk packets.

Small forests made up of twigs, branches and luxuriant leaves had been built over some of the wheelchairs. One child was hidden inside an elaborate hut that came fitted with a thatched roof.

Nanju's favourite was the Provision Store. His mother had rigged two sturdy sticks from either side of the wheelchair that supported a third horizontal one placed about two feet above his head. From this hung crushed chips packets, empty Eclair wrappers and squeezed-out tubes of toothpaste, along with a large empty yellow packet of Huggies, an empty container of washing powder

Nirma and a cylindrical bottle of Ponds cold cream. (Empty) packets of cigarettes—the pride of every self-respecting kaka shop—dangled everywhere.

To sit in the middle section was to be in the heart of all the action, with spitballs flying all over the place and the occasional punch thrown in for good measure. The prefects tried to patrol this area, yanking out a protesting offender and placing him in a different spot every once in a while. But as the afternoon wore on, they lost their initial enthusiasm and a jolly raucous equilibrium was restored.

A solid little fellow from Nursery with stubs for arms and a heart-shaped face framed by a jet-black fuzz, had burst onto the empty stage, belting out something that sounded more like a squeal than a song. Then before anyone could react, he bounded back into the oldest Ayamma's safe arms, where he got a hero's welcome.

'Why this Kolaveri Kolaveri di?' blared out again, and Vijay, a dwarf from Standard Six, took the floor. He was the Captain of the Yellow House and was a smart young man with a pronounced moustache.

Everyone instantly cheered up. Vijay danced. And danced. And danced.

One verse led into the other. The audience began to fidget. Eyes glazed over and a growing murmur of rebellion filled the room.

The show went on and on, and then at last it was time for the final act.

Kevin strolled on.

He'd insisted that he get the last spot and this demand had been conceded to in the best interest of the show.

Nanju's breath came faster and Ronit deigned to exchange a quick glance with him. Had Mahesh managed to catch Kevin in the act?

The older boy had had ample time to run into class and help himself to anything he fancied; Mahesh should have seen it all by now.

Nanju darted a quick look at Theresa Miss, who was sitting in her corner and trying not to yawn too obviously. She didn't seem to have heard from Mahesh yet.

Nanju looked at his watch. It was almost three o'clock and the bell would ring any minute now.

What had happened? And where was Mahesh?

Kevin, meanwhile, surveyed the crowd as they talked, laughed, fought and cried. Even the teachers were talking amongst themselves. No one was bothered about the performances anymore.

He nodded at the prefect who was manning the music system. The music came on and the show began.

It was a pantomime.

Kevin walked about, pretending to chew gum. He took the piece of gum out of his mouth and studied it, turning it around in his fingers. He tried to put it back in his mouth, but it was stuck to all the fingers of his right hand. He shook his hand. The gum stayed put. He frowned and shook his hand harder. It wouldn't budge.

He tugged at it with his other hand. Now it stuck to all his fingers. He shook his head in disbelief and looked up at the audience.

A loud cheer went up.

He finally got it off his left hand; it still clung firmly to the fingers of his right. He scratched his head, wondering what to do next.

It got stuck in his hair.

He groaned and the audience shrieked with laughter.

He really went to work then: carefully picking it out of each strand ... only for it to get stuck on his clothes.

At last, it came free.

It was now safely ensconced between his index finger and his thumb, and he gave a big smile of relief.

The room erupted in applause; even the teachers were clapping and smiling their approval.

It slipped from his fingers then—as he was about to pop it back into his mouth—and fell to the floor.

The crowd gasped.

Kevin looked down. Then he looked up. He shook his head sadly: time to give up.

He picked it up, brushed it lightly with his thumb, looked at everyone, shrugged his shoulders in a resigned fashion—and popped it back into his mouth.

He winked at the audience and walked off.

The bell rang and the show was over.

'Mahesh! What happened?'

Nanju had somehow pushed his way out of the school hall, packed with tired cranky children. He hadn't even waited for the results to be announced and had hobbled as fast as he could to class.

'What, man? Did you see him?' Ronit burst in as well.

Mahesh was sitting in his chair, his head lolling back, exhausted after spending two hours cooped up in a hot, scratchy basket. Tiny bits of straw were stuck in his hair that now stood up on end, making him look a little like a frazzled porcupine.

'No,' Mahesh shook his oversized head, stopped for a moment to sneeze a sneeze that threatened to blow his lungs out, and then continued. 'Nothing happened.'

'What do you mean?' Nanju asked. 'Didn't he come?'

'No. I watched the room for two hours—and no one came. It isn't Kevin.'

Monday, 11 August
(morning)

'Do you know why Theresa Miss has asked me to come to school today?' Appa spoke casually, as if it was an everyday occurrence for Theresa Miss to call and ask to see him.

He chuckled at Nanju's stricken face. 'Now don't look like that. She didn't sound angry or anything. Just said she wanted to meet all the parents today—before lunch break. Do you know why?'

'Don't know, Appa ...' Nanju mumbled.

'Don't you worry,' Appa ruffled his son's hair affectionately. Then, in the playful tone of voice that Nanju so hated: 'I've told your Prakash Mama to cancel your seat at the hostel ... so why should you worry, eh?'

A loud honk from the van rescued Nanju from the need to respond. He waved to Appa and flopped down into his seat, trying to make sense of what he'd just heard.

What could Theresa Miss possibly want to talk to Appa about?

Nanju knew, of course.

In just a few hours, Appa, Defender of the Innocent, Upholder of All Things Right, Saviour of Troubled Tailors would be informed that his son was a thief.

'But I swear I checked my bag before leaving the classroom on Friday, Miss!' Aradhana wailed.

It was the very first period and her maths notebook was missing.

'I changed out of my costume, came back to class and checked my bag before leaving for the van—and the book was there!'

'It must be at home, Aradhana. For god's sake, stop fussing about these books!' Theresa Miss leant against the blackboard for a minute and closed her eyes.

Maybe she'll faint, Nanju thought hopefully. Then the meeting with Appa would be called off.

Instead, Theresa Miss sat down and took out the attendance register.

'We had gone to my Aunty's house on the weekend, Miss. My father dropped me to school straight from her house this morning. I never took my books out at all!' Aradhana continued to whine.

'Then it can't disappear into thin air, can it?' Theresa Miss muttered through clenched teeth. 'Wait till I catch this troublemaker!'

And Nanju, sitting right up front, shivered a little.

Theresa Miss began to take attendance.

'Mona?'

'Absent, Miss,' the Class Monitor shouted back. It was his job to inform Theresa Miss of the absentees.

'Nanju?'

'Yes, Miss.'

'Miss! He's hurting, Miss!' someone complained from the back of the room.

'Stop it, Ronit!'

'He's still doing, Miss!' The statement culminated in a loud squeal.

'Ronit! Go to Principal's office! Pratik?'

'Absent, Miss,' the Class Monitor called again.

'Miss, I only poked with pencil, Miss!' an indignant Ronit tried to explain.

'Go! Now!' Theresa Miss yelled, kneading the skin between her eyebrows with great force.

Then to everyone's great joy, she muttered something about 'Going to office for tablet.' In a more normal tone, she barked, 'And copy down page 20 from the social science textbook till I come back! And be quiet!'

A loud cheer went up as soon as she left the room. Ronit made a u-turn—he had dragged himself as far as the door—and bounded back to his place. The others also lost no time in abandoning their seats. A happy mayhem engulfed the room.

'Nanju, lace has come out.' Mahesh liked to keep everything in order, including his shoelaces.

Nanju immediately slid to the ground and began to tie them together, a task that he did regularly as Mahesh's fingers couldn't quite manage tying knots. Then suddenly, he sat very still.

The speakers had not realised he was still in the room, as he sat at Mahesh's feet, hidden by the desks and chairs.

'No ya ... it's not him,' the familiar high-pitched voice insisted.

'I'm telling you, it is! She saw him!' Sangeetha's best friend replied vehemently. Sangeetha must be signing away beside her, thought Nanju.

'But why?'

'He's dumb! That's why!' was the answer.

'I still can't believe it ... Why would he want my books?'

'Just because he likes you, don't try and save him, okay?' another cheeky voice butted in.

'Chee! Why should I like him?' Aradhana answered, her voice indignant now. 'He's so stupid!'

The girls tittered and Aradhana's voice grew even angrier.

'Tell Miss then! Why should I care? Maybe he did take it!'

They were interrupted by a loud crash at the back of the room as Ronit came tumbling down a small mountain of chairs that he had stacked one on top of the other and had been trying to scale. Everyone rushed to the accident scene.

Nanju fumbled with Mahesh's shoelaces, his eyes blinded by tears. Without looking at Mahesh—he knew he too must have heard every single word—he mumbled something about the bathroom, staggered to his feet, and hobbled off.

'Who did you children like best?' Asha Miss asked.

They had finished with the session and it seemed only decent to spend some time dissecting the Talent Show that had happened the previous Friday.

'Kevin, Miss!'

'Then?'

'Aradhana, Miss.' Nanju's voice was muted, but he was faithful to the end.

'And what about your Class Monitor?'

The Class Monitor's speech about the 'Nine Golden Commandments of Being a Good Citizen' had been full of big words like commandments and citizen, and so no one had actually listened to him. But he had managed to get his speech out without too many pauses and there had even been a polite smattering of applause at the end.

'Dabba, Miss!' Ronit trashed his classmate.

'Miss, you record dance?' Kevin ran up to join them.

Kevin had won the Best Individual Performance and he had swaggered on to receive his prize. To his disgust, the prize had turned out to be a book.

'Provision Store' had won for Best Costume. Standard Four had won for Fancy Dress—all the children had come dressed as freedom fighters.

'Yes, I recorded it.' Asha Miss reached for her mobile phone. 'But why aren't you at your class picnic?'

Kevin's class had headed out that morning for the yearly picnic to the neighbourhood park.

'Came late, Miss. My Aunty not well so I went with her to doctor. Principal said to stay in school till others come back.'

'Oh, that's sad ...'

'No problem, Miss,' Kevin was studying the thirty-second recording closely.

He didn't seem upset, thought Nanju, but why should he be? He can do whatever he wants all day rather than rotting at some stupid picnic.

'That's all, Miss?' Kevin looked up.

'Yes, I couldn't see you clearly after this ... sorry.'

'It's okay, Miss.'

He ran off towards the playground.

Nanju watched Kevin leave with a heavy heart. Mahesh, too, was silent as he looked over at Nanju.

'Mahesh, why so quiet today? You're not feeling well again?' Asha Miss broke into his thoughts.

'No, Miss,' Mahesh answered.

But Nanju knew why he was quiet—Mahesh must be trying to make sense of just where Aradhana's book could have disappeared. Nanju had given up hope that the mystery could ever be solved; he would have to take the rap for it, that much was sure.

'So it's not Kevin, it's not Sangeetha, it's not Armaan, and Bhavani Amma was absent last Friday,' Mahesh spoke softly, to make sure no one in the classroom could hear him.

'The books keep turning up anyhow. Why should we care who's taking them?' Nanju answered rebelliously.

Things couldn't get worse—even Aradhana believed he was the thief—and so he had made his decision. If he was going to be sent away, it might as well be to a place of his choice. He was going to run away.

Break was over and they were back in class. Theresa Miss, however, had still not shown up. Rumours were flying thick and fast about a possible 'holiday', which meant that while no one could go home, there was no school work and they could pretty much do what they pleased.

The children had collected in little pockets around the classroom. Ronit, the Class Monitor and a few others were busy with a game of marbles. Some were sitting on top of their desks, their feet resting on their chairs as they played a game of Toss the Pen. Some of the girls were prattling away to one another.

Mahesh shot Nanju a quick look. He knew Nanju could well end up taking the blame for a crime he hadn't committed. The dangerous thing about rumours is that they sometimes morph into facts in people's minds, if they are repeated often enough. Mahesh had learnt this from watching the news every night on TV.

'Theresa Miss couldn't even finish taking the attendance,' Mahesh tried to change the topic in an attempt to restore normalcy. 'I must remind her that she stopped at P.'

Nanju, who was considering whether to run away by train or hitchhike his way to wherever it was he was running away to, missed the look of surprise that suddenly flashed across Mahesh's face. But he heard the excitement in Mahesh's voice as Mahesh pulled out his crumpled Criminal Calendar, now speckled with sambhar.

'The book was in her bag when Aradhana left on Friday—she said she checked it before she left for the van ... And she didn't take it out all weekend ... Only looked for it this morning as soon as she got into class. Someone must have taken it out of her bag between school and home.'

'But where?' Nanju couldn't resist asking. 'They couldn't have taken it from her house, could they?'

'Yes that's true,' Mahesh said. 'But still ...' He threw himself forward, stabbing his calendar as he contemplated the situation.

July 2014

Sun	Mon	Tue	Wed	Thurs	Fri	Sat
		1	2	3	4	5
6	7 A's science book found on wheelchain	8	9	10 A's maths book goes missing	11	12
13	14	15	16	17	18 A's maths book found in dustbin.	19 Suspects: Armaan, Sangeeta, Bhawani Amma & Karthik Uncle. Mer線 hate Aradhana
20	21	22 Suspects: Armaan off the list as cannot commit such a crime	23 No books missing this week → WHY?	24	25	26
27	28 A's English book goes missing	29	30	31 A & S fight		

Cricket match

August 2014

Sun	Mon	Tue	Wed	Thurs	Fri	Sat
					1 picnic +A absent	2
3	4 S's English book missing Key suspects: ??? Motive: ???	5	6 S's book found in classroom. Key suspect: Kevin Motive: Be a hero!	7	8 Talent show Trap Not Kevin! A's English book found in Theresa Miss's desk — pages ripped Key suspects: Sangeetha, but B Anna/K Uncle still on list	9
10	11 A's maths book goes missing	12	13	14	15	16
17	18	19	20	21	22	23
24	25	26	27	28	29	30
31						

Nanju reluctantly glanced at the calendar. He noticed that aside from the new entries, Mahesh had made some additional notes about Aradhana being absent on the day of the picnic, and had scrawled a big 'Why?' against the line that said no books went missing in the third week of July. As usual, it made no sense to him.

'Nanjegowda, come for therapy.'

The therapist rushed off to summon others. Nanju rose with a sigh—today even therapy couldn't cheer him up.

'Bye,' he mumbled to Mahesh, who nodded in a distracted manner.

As Nanju passed the nursery, it was with a heavy heart that he looked at the rosebushes and myriad pots of greens and blues and yellows—this might be the last time he would ever pass by this way. He would walk through the nursery: it didn't matter if anyone caught him or not, he was soon to be branded a criminal anyway.

He looked for Ramappa to say goodbye, but realised that this was the time for his tea break. He had already chatted with him in the morning, when Ramappa had grumbled about having to miss the Talent Show as there had been an unusually large number of customers at the nursery that Friday afternoon. He needed an assistant, Ramappa had sighed.

Nanju began with the purple begonias, sniffed at the unwieldy jasmine, then nicked a leaf off the pudina plant and popped it into his mouth. As he headed to the tall green palms with wide fronds that could hide a grown man, he suddenly realised that there was a grown man hiding behind them!

His instinctive reaction was to duck behind the chikoo tree.

Nanju wasn't renowned for his intellectual abilities, but he did have a fair amount of common sense that told him when something wasn't quite right.

He was greatly relieved to see that the man wasn't staring back at him but was looking in the opposite direction. Now that Nanju could observe him, he seemed quite young, more of a boy, with hair that had been shorn into a pattern of fancy swirls just above his ears. His ears were packed tight with earrings and around his chest there was a thick silver chain with a black metal skull.

Where is everyone, Nanju wondered. Then he remembered that most of the school was in class or at the picnic. The therapists would be busy inside the Centre, and Ramappa was off for his tea break.

The boy began to mouth something, still looking at the opposite end. He must have someone with him! He jerked his thumb towards the school gates that were a short walk away from whoever he was addressing at that end of the nursery.

The boy slowly bent down and picked up a big plastic garbage bag. A few green stems popped out of it, and the boy hastily shoved them back in.

They're stealing from the nursery, Nanju realised with a shock. He knew some of the plants were fairly expensive and were sold at hundreds of rupees; one could sell them outside and make a neat packet.

The boy was still signalling to his accomplice at the far end and Nanju craned his neck to try and locate him. Then the accomplice rose to his feet and Nanju's heart came to an abrupt stop.

'Few more ...' Kevin hissed to the boy, pointing at a row of expensive ficus that were lined up across where the boy was hidden.

The boy consulted his watch and nodded. Kevin began to creep forward.

So this was why Kevin had come in late to school this morning, Nanju thought, and the pieces of the puzzle began to fall in place, first slowly, and then faster and faster: click, click, click!

Kevin had meant to miss the picnic all along so that he could stay back and work uninterrupted.

This was the 'special' thing he had boasted about to his friends.

Kevin must have planned to do a big haul of plants on the afternoon of the Talent Show—Ramappa was always a regular at the school performances. But his plan had been foiled as Ramappa had not been able to go.

Kevin wasn't taking Aradhana's books. He was, instead, helping himself to something much more profitable.

Nanju considered.

Ramappa would be at this very moment sitting just around the corner, blissfully unaware that his precious plants were being spirited away in large garbage bags. Nanju could stand by and allow Kevin and that nasty young creep to finish, and then report the matter to Ramappa. This made the most sense as he wouldn't be risking life and limb—Kevin could get really nasty at the first sign of being discovered.

But then there was Ramappa to consider.

Who would believe Nanju's story of Kevin and some mysterious outsider making away with bagfuls of plants? And that too under Ramappa's very nose! Ramappa would be the one to fall under suspicion.

Nanju looked around him; if someone was passing by he could jump out and tell them everything. But the path was empty.

Nanju hesitated for a moment. He thought of Ramappa lovingly tending to his plants. And he knew what he had to do.

He took a deep breath and stepped out.

'Ay Kevin, what you're doing man?' Nanju's voice sounded very un-Nanju like even to his own ears—more like a high-pitched trembly squeak.

Kevin straightened like a shot. From the corner of his eye, Nanju could see the plants begin to rustle where the other boy was hiding.

'Helping Ramappa, you idiot—then what?' Kevin barked. His voice didn't sound as assured as it always did.

He shot a quick look at where his accomplice was hidden and Nanju followed his eyes.

The creep was moving now, but sideways, as if to beat a hasty retreat.

'But where is Ramappa?' Nanju choked out.

This time, Kevin took a step forward.

'Go from here, Nanjegowda,' he said in a low voice and reached out and pushed him in the chest. Nanju staggered backwards but somehow managed to retain his precarious balance. He looked to the tall plants again and saw that the boy had reached the end of the nursery and was preparing to make a dash for the gate.

'Ramappa! Ramappa! Come soon!' Nanju suddenly hollered at the top of his voice.

Kevin made a snarling sound and pushed Nanju to the ground. Nanju fell with a hard thud. He couldn't get up—his legs were twisted in a funny way—but all the while he could hear himself shout, as if from some far-off place: 'Ramappa! Ramappa! Come soon!'

'Shut up!' Kevin gave Nanju a few sharp kicks. He grabbed the bag of plants off the ground and ran to follow his friend.

Ramappa, surprisingly agile for a man with two uneven legs, bounded over and grabbed his arm.

'What are you doing, Kevin?' Ramappa shouted. He spotted the thief who was heading for the gate at full tilt: 'Ay stop! Thief! Thief!'

Kevin twisted violently and almost broke away, when one of the therapists, hearing all the shouting, ran out of the Centre and grabbed him by the shoulders.

The other boy, however, had run out of the gate, turned the corner, and was out of sight.

Nanju lay sprawled on the ground, the flaps on his dusty calipers undone, not feeling the least bit heroic.

Ramappa had brusquely ordered him back to class. He had his hands full with Kevin, who was writhing like a python. They had all left for Principal's office and Nanju was alone again.

Nanju managed to slowly right himself, limped over to a bench, and sat down. He counted his bruises: scrapes on each knee—one was bleeding quite nicely—and a rather painful left buttock where Kevin had delivered two well-placed kicks. All in all, though, he would live.

A growing sense of something warm and delicious enveloped him: like someone had tipped him over and filled him up with a bag of sunshine.

After what seemed to him like a long time, Nanju got up and decided to make his way back to class. He was still feeling all warm and fuzzy when he saw Ronit charging up the path, yelling for him.

'Where are you, man?' Ronit braked to a halt inches away from Nanju. 'Theresa Miss is calling—she's very angry! And your Appa too has come.' He gave Nanju a victorious smile. 'You're going to get it this time.'

'Shutyamouth!' Nanju mumbled, the blaze of contentment evaporating at supersonic speed.

'Nanju!' Theresa Miss was standing outside class on the pathway. She can't even wait for me to come inside, Nanju thought bitterly. 'Where were you?'

Appa stood beside her. Mahesh was parked in his wheelchair beside Appa.

'Therapy, Miss,' he mumbled, unable to meet Appa's eyes. 'But Miss ...'

'I go away for five minutes and everyone is all over the place! Mahesh roaming all over school with that shaky Sushil pushing him—no wonder they both nearly fell into the ditch! And the others turning the classroom inside out! And you go and disappear when you know your father is coming!'

'Sorry, Miss ...'

'And Mahesh giving tall tales about Aradhana's books ... Do you know anything about it?'

Nanju shook his head, slightly confused at where the conversation was headed. He looked at Mahesh, who was looking a tad dishevelled. But his eyes were shining and he seemed very pleased with himself.

'Miss, it can only be him,' Mahesh spoke up in his slow deliberate way.

Theresa Miss hesitated.

Appa said, 'I will come with you, Miss. You may need help.'

'Go where, Appa?' Nanju was thoroughly bewildered. Something was going on, but for some heaven-sent reason, he wasn't at the centre of it.

'You two go back to class,' Theresa Miss ordered. 'I will come soon.'

Monday, 11 August (afternoon)

Nanju spent the rest of the day in a state of high frustration.

Mahesh refused to tell him what was happening. He said he had promised Theresa Miss not to say anything till she was back.

'But I told you about Kevin, no?' Nanju demanded angrily. 'I could have also kept quiet!'

But it was useless.

Mahesh was impressed with Nanju's story and made him repeat it a few times, which took the sting out of his refusal a little.

Then, just when Nanju had given up all hope—the school bell had rung and he was shoving things into his bag—Theresa Miss entered the classroom.

'Bye Miss ... bye Miss ...' a happy medley of voices called out as the children left for the day. It had been by far the best day Standard Five had had this year.

Only Nanju and Mahesh stayed put.

Theresa Miss sat down on her chair and stared at her desk.

'Miss,' Mahesh spoke. 'Van will leave soon ...'

Theresa Miss nodded.

'You were right,' she finally looked up. Both boys were taken aback by how old their class teacher suddenly looked.

'It was Pratik.'

Pratik's Daddy believed in keeping an eye on his son.

This he did by checking his schoolwork once a week after a stiff drink at the neighbourhood bar, his weekly wages safely tucked away in to his back pocket. He would shout at the boy to show him his books, and pore over them to look for red marks, the telltale signs that confirmed to him how useless his son was.

'Let him be, Pa,' Pratik's mother would try to intervene. 'He'll settle down slowly. After all, we put him in this school so that he might learn at a slow pace.'

But his father was having none of it.

Bad times had forced them out of their home to the city. Only he knew the humiliation he had to face on a daily basis, hauling bricks around constructions sites, all the while being ordered around, shouted at, abused like a dog on the street.

Well, his son would do better than that. He would make sure of it.

Terrified of what would happen to him if he continued to show his father his own books—with their smattering of red crosses to highlight the careless mistakes he made on a regular basis—Pratik decided on a plan. He would help himself to the books of the cleverest student in class and give them back as soon as his father had finished with them. He knew his father would be too drunk to realise the handwriting might not be his son's.

From his seat right behind her in the van, it was a matter of moments to stick his hand into Aradhana's bag—which she carelessly tossed on the floor as soon as she got in—and pull out a book and quickly shove it into his own bag.

Aradhana was always so busy chatting and laughing with some friend, happy to be done with another day at school—as were all the other kids on the van—that neither she nor anyone else ever noticed him.

Mahesh later explained to Nanju that a stray comment about Theresa Miss stopping at P in the attendance register had set his mind whirling. Pratik was the only student whose name started with that letter.

He had suddenly thought of Pratik in the van, sitting behind Sangeetha, in what was originally Aradhana's place, and he had known: the only place the books could have been taken from, was the van.

Mahesh had crosschecked his calendar to be sure, and had realised that when Pratik's father had been away for a week—he remembered Theresa Miss shouting at Pratik for shaving off his eyebrows around this time—no books had been taken!

Pratik had to be the one who was behind the missing books. Though he had not known why.

When he had explained his theory to Theresa Miss, she had rushed off to Pratik's house, anxious about why he hadn't come to school that day.

'And my worst fears were confirmed ...' Theresa Miss faltered, and for a terrible moment Nanju thought she was going to cry.

She had so far spoken in a low, flat tone of voice, quite unlike her usual outbursts. Nanju decided he didn't like this new style very much.

To his great relief, she swallowed hard, took a moment, and continued: 'This morning, his father realised that the maths book was not his and ... and beat him very badly. He's in the hospital now—your Appa helped me take him there.'

Nanju's heart swelled with pride. But he waited impatiently for Theresa Miss to continue.

'He's very badly hurt ...' A tear escaped down Theresa Miss's thin cheek and she didn't bother to brush it away. 'The rod broke his leg ... and a hand. But his mother is with him in the hospital. They will take care of him now.'

'And his father, Miss?' Mahesh whispered.

'Run away. Thought he had ...'

'But why, Miss? Why did his father do that?' and to

his great embarrassment, Nanju burst out crying. He was no fan of Pratik, but he couldn't bear to think of him lying bruised and broken in a hospital bed.

'Sometimes people do things they don't mean to ...' Theresa Miss wiped her eyes and drew Nanju close. Mahesh was crying softly as well and she leaned over and put her arm around his fragile shoulders.

Pratik's father bought him nice things every now and again, Theresa Miss continued, though she said, almost as if to herself, this was normally after a particularly violent beating. A new schoolbag, a flashy pair of cheap sports shoes. During his saner moments, he was a loving, even indulgent man, who was genuinely concerned for his son's future.

But it was when he stumbled home at night, drunk out of his mind and itching to take out the frustration of his long, never-ending day, on someone, anyone, that the monster emerged.

Theresa Miss explained that she had begun to suspect abuse of some sort a while ago. Her last meeting with Pratik's mother had not been about Pratik kicking the Class Monitor in the ribs, but about the constant signs of violence that had begun to worry her: a burn mark on an arm, a bruised nose, swollen feet.

'I knew something wasn't right at the picnic, when Pratik refused to play and just sat on the bench and watched you all. He said his feet were paining and I stupidly believed ...'

What had really happened was that a few days before the picnic Karthik Uncle had complained to Pratik's father about the boy walking home the previous week instead of using school transport. Pratik's father had made his son take off his shoes and kneel down, and then caned him on the soles of his feet with a long, thin stick.

'This was why he had been absent for three days before the picnic ...' Theresa Miss's voice dropped away.

Nobody said anything. In the background, the school vans revved their engines, the first warning that they would be leaving soon.

The Monday after the picnic, Theresa Miss had noticed the cut above Pratik's lip and had summoned Pratik's mother, warning her that if the beatings didn't stop the school would take action. She had hoped that Pratik's mother would scare her husband off. But his mother had been too scared to even mention it to Pratik's father.

'That's why I asked your Appa to come in today,' Theresa Miss looked at Nanju, her eyes sad. 'I wanted to talk to all the parents of my class—about the need to handle you children with love and care. Not like this ...'

How silly of Theresa Miss to think Appa would ever treat him badly!

'But how did his father not guess the books were not Pratik's?' Nanju wiped his nose on his sleeve. Theresa Miss would have normally pulled him up for forgetting his handkerchief yet again, but this time she didn't even notice.

'He took off the book's jacket—that had Aradhana's name on it—and slipped on a jacket from his own book so that his father would think the book was his.'

Aradhana wouldn't have written her name inside her book because Theresa Miss was manic about such things—and from their faces, it looked like Mahesh and Theresa Miss were also thinking the same—but no one said anything and the moment passed.

'Then, once his father had finished going through the book, he switched the covers and brought it back,' Theresa Miss finished.

'That's why the books were returned in such a shabby state,' Nanju said, his heart going out to poor, frightened Pratik.

'Yes, his father was the one who ripped those pages out of Aradhana's book. He was really angry that day after Karthik had complained to him about Pratik not using the van. Pratik had also shaved off his eyebrows that week—that only made things worse.'

Theresa Miss fell silent for a moment, before continuing: 'But then Aradhana did write her name in one of the books after all—on the last page, in pencil. She must have meant to rub it out later and forgotten all about it. Pratik's father saw it this morning and guessed what he was up to ...'

Nanju marvelled at this new and improved version of Theresa Miss, talking to them as if they were friends and not her students.

He decided to take advantage of the situation and ask another question. 'But why did Pratik take only one book, Miss? Why not more than one?'

Theresa Miss said she didn't know the answer to this question, but she guessed that it was because Pratik didn't want to take too much of a risk.

'Maybe he didn't want Aradhana to suffer too much ...' Nanju suggested, and was slightly miffed when Mahesh and Theresa Miss looked noncommittal.

Pratik also left all his own notebooks in his desk in school; his schoolbag was full of textbooks and the single notebook he filched every week.

'And then Kevin,' Mahesh piped up, with something like a smile in his voice. 'We thought he threw Aradhana's book back into class because he heard me asking Asha Miss about robbers being punished, and got scared.'

Yes!' Nanju remembered this well. He quickly explained the details to Theresa Miss, who nodded morosely.

'But what must have actually happened was that Pratik, who had been returning from the toilet at that time, overheard our conversation, and he got scared and threw the book in during lunchtime.' The smile had gone out of Mahesh's voice now.

As for Kevin, they now knew that he had been frightened off because he thought they were alluding to his work in the Nursery.

'No wonder his behaviour was so ...' Theresa Miss sighed. 'And he was a clever boy actually—didn't need half those tuitions his father packed him off for. Poor boy.'

The vans roared their imminent departure and Theresa Miss rose slowly from her chair.

'Come children, let's go.'

She picked up her battered old handbag and wheeled Mahesh out of the door, Nanju hobbling behind as fast as he could.

Two weeks later, Theresa Miss took Nanju, Mahesh and Ronit aside and told them that Pratik, his baby sister Blessy and their mother were headed back to their small town to live with Pratik's grandparents.

Pratik's father had disappeared and had not been seen since that fateful day.

Pratik couldn't walk yet, Theresa Miss said. The beating had fractured his thigh and broken two bones in his upper arm, and his face was still puffy and bruised. But he was happy to be going home to the grandparents who adored him.

Pratik hadn't been able to come back to school or meet his friends before leaving, but Theresa Miss said that he had whispered to her in the hospital to apologise to Aradhana and Sangeetha on his behalf and tell them how sorry he was for taking their books. He also wanted Ronit to have his Ben 10 bag.

'Tell him bye, Miss. Tell him I won't forget him.'

Monday, 15 September

Nanju shifted from foot to foot as he waited at Principal's desk, holding on to the back of the chair for support.

It was hard for him to stand for more than ten minutes at a time, all the while shifting from foot to foot. But he routinely shrugged aside all suggestions to use a walker. The therapist had explained to him that as he grew older, his muscles would tighten further, and he would find it harder to do all the things he did now. But Nanju's motto was why worry about tomorrow when today was so wonderful, and he didn't let these kinds of things bother him.

'Nanjegowda, do you know why I called for you?' Principal looked up from the papers on her desk and trained fierce eyes on him. 'And sit down please!'

Nanju perched himself at the edge of the chair.

Principal was looking particularly fetching in a midnight-blue saree that had a very large green and gold peacock feather stretching from her left shoulder to somewhere below the desk.

'I called you because I wanted to tell you a story.'

Principal sat back and surveyed Nanju, who instantly began to feel like a mouse on the radar of a rather hungry bird.

'I want to tell you a story about a boy whose father doesn't care for him, and whose mother works as a maid in a country far away, so that he might have a better life. A boy who has no one to guide or support him, who falls into wrong company and does something stupid, because he thinks that's the only way he can do better.'

She paused. 'Do you know who that boy is?'

Nanju hated such questions. How in the world should he know who this stupid fellow was?

He shook his head.

'Kevin.' Principal sat forward and folded her arms on her desk. 'As you know, after that ... incident, which, by the way, I warned you not to talk about. Did you tell anyone?'

'No, Miss.'

Except for Mahesh and Ronit and Aradhana and Sushil and maybe Sangeetha—he couldn't be sure—he had not told anyone.

'Good. As you might have noticed, Kevin wasn't in school for a while—but he will be back from today. And now that I hope you understand how hard his life is, I want you to be kind to him and behave normally. There is to be no more talk about what happened in the nursery that day. Do you understand, Nanjegowda?'

Nanju bobbed his head vigorously to indicate he understood.

'Ah, Zafar and Junaid,' Principal looked past Nanju at the door. 'Come in boys, you're late.'

Nanju swung around to see the two second-graders inch into the room.

When the dust had settled, Ramappa had told Nanju that Kevin had been stealing plants from the nursery for a while, and selling them in the slum for small sums of money. His carriers had been Zafar and Junaid, who had been threatened with violence if they dared to resist.

Nanju and Asha Miss had, in fact, caught them in the act when they had been on their way to the Therapy Centre that day. The boys had been hurrying, booty in hand, to pass on to Kevin, who was waiting outside the school gates.

Ramappa said that Zafar and Junaid had been let off with a stern warning. Kevin, however, had been suspended for a month and had narrowly escaped being sent to a juvenile detention home.

'His mother had to leave her job and fly down from Dubai to beg Principal not to report him to the authorities,' Ramappa shook his head. 'Otherwise, gone! And he wouldn't tell who that other fellow was—however much his mother beat him, he just wouldn't tell.'

'And to think I caught him, Ramappa!' Nanju was still amazed at his courage that day.

And Ramappa had smiled and agreed, 'Yes Nanju, you only caught him.'

'Sorry Mizz,' Zafar adjusted his dark glasses for better protection from the bright sunlight that flooded Principal's room. Junaid stood to attention on his boot-encased knees. Both scanned the room for signs of their old boss and looked relieved to find he wasn't there.

'Hope you boys are behaving yourselves?'

Nanju zoned out for a bit, as Principal droned on about Kevin for the benefit of the younger boys. It was all very well for Kevin to have a tough life, but Nanju was more worried about how he would be made to pay for it when Kevin got back.

A familiar voice called out, 'Good morning, Miss', and Kevin strode into the room.

'Come, Kevin,' Principal nodded to him in a firm but kind manner.

Kevin walked up to her desk, giving Nanju and his ex-crew a quick what-are-you-lot-doing-over-here kind of look.

Nanju, who had almost fallen off the chair at this dramatic entry, allowed himself to slide back a bit. Zafar and Junaid had shrunk like the touch-me-nots they terrorised regularly in the nursery.

'I think you have something to say to these children, right, Kevin?' Principal looked at him.

'Yes, Miss.'

Kevin turned to all three parties, and, in the manner of a master bestowing largesse on his slaves, said: 'I'm sorry.'

'Good,' Principal sounded relieved. 'Now I want you all to be friends. And there should be no more reports of any kind of trouble, you understand?'

A wave of nods filled the room.

'And tell your mother to come and meet me before she goes back to Dubai,' Principal addressed Kevin.

'She went Dubai, Miss. Next day only. And she gave money also.'

He whipped out a shiny brown wallet from his pocket and opened it with a flourish. Nestled within were at least three brand-new hundred-rupee notes.

'My mother gave,' he repeated proudly, pointing to a passport-sized picture of a smiling, round-faced woman in a saree. Giving the picture one last look, he closed the wallet and put it back into his pocket.

'Left the next day! But she said she would stay at least a month—till you were back in school ... and so much money!'

'She only gave, Miss! She said she will send more also.'

Principal sighed. 'Sit down, Kevin. I need to talk to you. And you others, go back to class.'

'Yes, Miss.' Kevin made himself comfortable and began to survey the room with great interest. One never knew where the next opportunity might lie.

Nanju bounded out of the room, followed by the equally fast-footed duo, all happy to be let out of the lion's den.

His deepest thoughts were perfectly echoed by Zafar, who stoically remarked: 'He'll beat now.'

But right now, the sun was out and the playground was full of children making the last of the snack break. Zafar and Junaid raced off to play a quick game of hide-and-seek and Nanju hurried to the bench where Mahesh waited for him.

The courtyard was bursting at the seams with noisy boisterous children as the countdown for the last precious moments of freedom began.

'Dum laga ke haiya!' the Class Monitor's younger brother yelled, as he spun the wheels of his wheelchair with all his might and zipped across the courtyard like a race car. His left leg was swaddled in layers of bandages. He had just recovered from another fracture and was back in school after a gap of four weeks.

'Stop! Stop!'

His older brother chased after the wheelchair in a very un-Class-Monitor-like manner.

Trring!

Nanju reached the bench just as the bell ended. Ronit was with Mahesh.

Theresa Miss had suggested to Principal that the little group that had helped solve the case be given a small reward. Mahesh, Nanju, and Ronit (more in lieu of being Pratik's best friend) had been declared Prefects-in-Training for a whole term.

'Why so late?' Ronit snapped at Nanju.

Ronit was in charge of chasing the last few stragglers out of the playground, and he took off without waiting for an answer.

Nanju grabbed Mahesh's wheelchair and whizzed him over to the point just outside the lunch hall. Not too many kids congregated there during break; this was a manageable spot for his friend.

Then he hobbled over to the head of the alley that led from the courtyard to the boys' toilet. This was a particularly notorious area that needed strict patrolling.

He was pretty sure this was indicative of just how highly the management thought of him and he couldn't help but swell up with pride.

'Get back to class!' Nanju barked at a smart aleck who strolled up the alley.

From the corner of his eye, he saw Aradhana throw him an admiring look as she made her way to class, her arm linked with Sangeetha's.

The old Nanju would have flashed her a grateful grin. The new one pretended he hadn't noticed and continued to train his attention on the suspect.

He was rewarded with a last wistful look before Aradhana disappeared into the corridor.

The wastrel had wet his hair under a tap in the washbasin and had stroked it upwards into spikes. Droplets of water ran down his sunburnt face.

The boy stopped and stared at Nanju. Who are you, his eyes seemed to say.

Nanju's heart skipped a beat. He looked around to see if he could call for reinforcements—if there was to be a showdown, he was not at all sure that he would come out victorious.

But courtyard had emptied out and there wasn't a soul in sight.

Nanju took a deep breath.

'Come on! Hurry up!' he shouted in his best Prefect voice. 'Don't waste my time!'

And the boy took one last look at him, and hurried off.

Zainab Sulaiman is a special educator who has taught and raised funds in the non-profit sector. She enjoys writing fiction and hanging out with people far wiser than her, namely her children.